Jill didn't know why—maybe it was the amused expression on Remy's face—but she was feeling the stirrings of pure panic. Yet Remy wasn't acting as if they'd just been poisoned! Quite the opposite. He studied his glass, then took another sip.

Jill gasped. "What *is* this?"

"Sure you want to know, sugar?" Remy's eyes sparkled with mischief.

Somehow, Jill found his attitude more disturbing than the vile taste of the liquid she'd downed so naively. "What?"

"This might be a case where ignorance is truly bliss," he warned.

"Tell me!"

"Sugar, unless I'm mistaken—" Remy grinned "—you are now under the influence of the irresistible, very famous, ultrapotent, Love Potion #5.

ABOUT THE AUTHOR

Cathy Gillen Thacker is a full-time novelist who once taught piano to children. Born and raised in Ohio, she attended Miami University. After moving cross-country several times, she settled in Texas with her husband and three children.

Books by Cathy Gillen Thacker

HARLEQUIN AMERICAN ROMANCE

HARLEQUIN INTRIGUE

Don't miss any of our special offers. Write to us at the following address for information on our newest releases.

Harlequin Reader Service
U.S.: 3010 Walden Ave., P.O. Box 1325, Buffalo, NY 14269
Canadian: P.O. Box 609, Fort Erie, Ont. L2A 5X3

Cathy Gillen Thacker

LOVE POTION #5

Harlequin Books

TORONTO • NEW YORK • LONDON
AMSTERDAM • PARIS • SYDNEY • HAMBURG
STOCKHOLM • ATHENS • TOKYO • MILAN
MADRID • WARSAW • BUDAPEST • AUCKLAND

ISBN 0-373-16556-0

LOVE POTION #5

Chapter One

"So how much is this going to cost me?" Jill Sutherland demanded as she strode impatiently out onto the snowy white veranda of Magnolia Place, her great-aunt's plantation home.

All around, fragrant pink, red, white and lavender azaleas heralded the spring, but it was the beauty in front of him that captured Remy's attention. She was something, all right, with that soft sexy cap of mahogany hair and those big blue eyes. It was just too bad she was one of those gotta-have-a-schedule-and-keep-to-it-at-all-times types.

"That all depends," Remy drawled as he slouched against the railing on the veranda. He crossed one blue-jeaned leg over the other, pushed his Cajuns Do It All Better bill cap farther back on his head, and surveyed her in leisurely fashion. As the hot, annoyed color rose in her pretty cheeks, his grin widened. He could never resist playing with these workaholic types. "How much do you want it to cost you?" he deadpanned mischievously.

As expected, Jill heaved an impatient sigh that indicated she had counted every moment of the one hour, five minutes and forty-two seconds he had been late to their appointment. She regarded him with flashing eyes and a thin-lipped smile. "Listen, Mr.—"

"Beauregard. Remy Beauregard. But you can call me Remy if you like, sugar."

Jill Sutherland sent a glance heavenward. "I haven't got time for this, Mr. Beauregard," she announced in a low, clipped tone that only made him desire her all the more.

"I know." Remy stopped flirting long enough to add sympathetically, "You've got a sick great-aunt to tend."

"And next year's bible to write," Jill muttered impatiently. She stalked closer, her three-inch red heels making staccato sounds on the pristine white porch floor.

Remy frowned. He didn't have the slightest idea what she was talking about. "Next year's...what?"

"Bible. I write for a soap opera. Oh, never mind." She waved her hand dismissively. "How long is it going to take for you to give me an estimate?"

Remy let his eyes drift over her figure, luxuriating in its sensual curves and hollows. There were dozens of places he wanted to explore to the fullest, but there was not much chance he'd get the opportunity. Lifting his eyes back to her face, he offered an insolent grin. "You city girls sure are in a hurry."

"And you Cajun fellas sure are not!"

Remy chuckled. "You always been this way?" he asked, appreciating the way she looked in her fancy outfit. The long red tunic clung to her breasts, deliciously outlining the soft full globes, then glided gracefully past her slender waist and on down to her delectably curvy derriere. The matching skirt beneath it was slim, sexy and ended a good four inches above her knees. Remy reluctantly returned his gaze to her face. "Or just since you moved to the Big Apple?" he teased.

Her dark blue eyes flashed. "Always," she snapped.

Remy wondered what it would be like to have those same eyes close in surrender as she prepared to receive his kiss, and whether he would ever know. He decided he would, if he had his way. "Too bad," he sympathized bluntly as he removed his aviator sunglasses and slid them into the breast pocket of his starched white oxford cloth shirt. "Life goes down better if you slow down. You oughta relax and enjoy it some, sugar, instead of just running around like a cat with his tail on fire."

Rosy color flowed into her high, delicately boned cheeks. "Mr. Beauregard, whether or not I enjoy my life is my business, not yours!"

"That's also true, sugar," Remy nodded in mock solemnness.

Jill propped her hands on her slender waist. She leaned forward until they were nearly nose to nose and he could smell her delicate rose perfume. "But just for the record," she said, her low voice crackling with aggravation, "I'm sure I wouldn't know what it's like to slow down to the rate you suggest. Nor do I want to know, since you seem to work at a snail's pace."

Remy watched her pivot and march back to the front door. Her hips swayed provocatively beneath the short skirt and curvaceous muscles flexed in her calves. More taken with her than he had ever been with any other woman, he began to laugh. Damn, but she had a fiery temper and a sharp tongue to match. "I think I'm going to like this job," he murmured.

Jill whirled, her hand on the door. She arched a discriminating mahogany brow. "Who said you had it?"

Remy got to his feet. "Your great-aunt Hildy, of course. I talked to her at the hospital this morning. She said you'd be a handful. She was right." He moved past her and walked inside, passing a gold-edged mirror, an antique parson's table and priceless Oriental rug, up the sweeping front staircase and into the upstairs hall.

Jill followed reluctantly.

"First thing we got to do is take care of this place where Hildy fell," he said. "She might've been able to handle the lights suddenly going out on her if she hadn't caught the toe of her house slipper on the edge of this. That's what made her trip and fall." Remy knelt to examine the priceless three-foot-wide carpet. "This runner ought to be tacked down." He replaced it and straightened again. "I can do that, too, if you like."

"I'll handle the tacking, thanks," Jill said stiffly.

"Sure, sugar?" Remy grinned. "It'd be no trouble."

Jill glared at him. "Let's get a couple things straight, Mr. Beauregard. My name is not Sugar." Her shoulders stiff with aggravation, Jill pivoted and marched back down the stairs. Remy followed her.

Jill crossed to the parlor. A laptop computer sat on an antique writing desk and a stack of papers was beside it. "And don't try to bulldoze me with your countrified manner, Mr. Beauregard. Aunt Hildy said you have a degree in electrical engineering from LSU."

"That's right. Before I decided I liked working with wiring more than I liked designing it. There's just something about using your hands," Remy drawled. "But then, you probably know what I mean." He indicated an ink smudge on her fingertip.

Jill jerked her hand from his. She tended to get ink on her hands whenever she wrote out her story ideas longhand. It was rude of him to point it out.

She sent him a stony look. "I want you to stop this right now," she ordered firmly.

Remy regarded her with wide-eyed innocence. "You're telling me you *want* to go around with ink smudges all over your fingers?"

Jill lifted an ink-stained fingertip and waved it under his nose. "I am telling you, you can cut the Cajun charm, lover boy, because it is not, and I repeat, it is *not* going to work on me. I have no intention of letting you flirt your way into my good graces. Particularly not after the way you kept me waiting!"

Remy leaned in close, until they were a mere fraction of an inch apart and he could feel the heat of her body. "What makes you think I want to be in your good graces?" he chided softly, figuring it was past time she found out he could give back every bit as good as he got.

"I know your type," she said quietly, her dark blue eyes turning suddenly remote and vulnerable. She looked down at the legal pad in front of her. "Now on to the estimate. Aunt Hildy said the lights in the upstairs hall are short-circuiting."

"Unfortunately, sugar, it's a safe guess there are electrical problems everywhere else, too. Since everything's connected, it won't do any good to simply fix one circuit. I've got to check them all out, and probably, for safety's sake—since the wiring in Magnolia Place is so old—replace them."

She blinked, wary of the time involved for such a chore. "You're suggesting you completely rewire the house?" That would take days!

Remy nodded. "As soon as possible, if you've got the cash for the materials."

"Which should amount to approximately how much?" Jill asked.

He shrugged. "Let's have a look and see." Remy took a quick tour of the place, Jill nipping at his heels the whole way, then returned downstairs. Getting out his calculator, he quickly estimated how much wire would be required to outfit all twelve rooms in the beautifully kept-up home. Finished, he ripped off the top sheet and handed her the paper with his calculations. "That's what we'll need for material." Because she looked wary of him, he added, "Don't worry. I won't rob your aunt or overcharge her."

Jill's dark blue glance narrowed. "You mean you won't rob me. I'm footing the bill for this, starting with the materials." She glanced up at him, her expression serious. If she realized he was giving her the materials at cost, she showed no sign of it. "How much are we talking about in terms of labor?"

Remy admired the way she was trying to protect her great-aunt's interests, financial and otherwise, but it was hardly necessary. "I'm donating my time, nights and weekends. I'll have to work around my paying jobs, but I figure I've got plenty of time to finish the job before Hildy comes home from the hospital."

"What's your angle?"

"I don't have one."

"Well, I can't have you do this for no charge."

"Why not?" Remy ambled over to the sofa and made himself at home. "Hildy doesn't mind."

"Hildy isn't thinking clearly now." Jill followed him reluctantly and sat down in a chair opposite him.

"*Hildy's* thinking is just fine. You're the one with the problem. Why are you so hell-bent on taking charge of the repairs, anyway? Hildy usually handles her own affairs."

Jill crossed her legs at the knee and tugged her skirt down as far as it would go. Not that it did much good. Remy could still see a good six inches of slender thigh. "I'm trying to be helpful," she said.

Remy didn't doubt that for a minute. The problem was, Jill was taking the wrong approach. As Hildy's friend, it was up to him to convince her of that. "I know how close the two of you are," he commiserated softly. "Hildy says you call her all the time, and that you wish you could get back to see her for more than just a weekend every few months." But Jill's work as head writer of a popular daytime soap required that she be in New York much of the time.

Jill frowned, her unhappiness with the situation evident. "It hasn't been easy, living so far away," she admitted.

"I know," Remy said. Jill sent him a questioning look, compelling Remy to elaborate casually, "Whenever I stop by for Sunday dinner, you're all Hildy talks about. Have I seen the show? Did I see you win your Emmy?"

Jill sat back in her chair. She crossed her arms in front of her and regarded Remy suspiciously. "How often do you eat Sunday dinner here?"

"Before she fell, every week."

"I see. And how long has this been going on?"

Remy was beginning to feel like a witness being cross-examined on the stand, but he kept his tone casual as he answered, "About six months ago, shortly after I bought the place next door. It all started when I began driving her to church. You knew about that, didn't you? How she plowed her car into the shrubbery?" Remembering, he shook his head.

"Yes." Jill's expression was troubled. "I even offered to hire her a driver after she lost her license."

"But she wouldn't hear of it," Remy supplied.

Jill sighed and threw up her hands in exasperation. "She said she could rely on her friends just fine." She gave Remy a pointed look. "If I'd have known what friends she meant, I would have hired her a driver anyway."

Remy grinned. "Does this mean you don't approve of me?"

Jill got up to pace the room once again. "Bingo."

Remy followed her. "Why not?"

Jill stalked back to her laptop computer and idly fingered the keys. She wouldn't meet his gaze. "I would think that would be clear enough."

Remy moved in close. "Explain it anyway," he prodded softly.

Jill scowled down at her keyboard. "Aunt Hildy needs a man she can trust working on Magnolia Place."

Remy frowned. He wasn't sure whether Jill had meant to insult him or not, but she had. "She can trust me," he said flatly.

Jill pivoted slightly and tipped her face up to his. Their eyes held. "I'll be the judge of that."

Remy studied her silently. He didn't know what had happened to Jill to make her so wary, but he vowed he would find out. "Yes, I expect you will," he said.

Silence fell between them as their glances continued to collide. Finally, Jill stiffened, stepped back and turned away from him. "Back to the job. It's important the house be fixed to Aunt Hildy's liking, even if she can no longer continue to live here alone."

"Does this mean you plan to move back and keep her company? If so, I approve." Remy winked at her and continued to follow her as she restlessly paced the room. "You'll have great neighbors."

Jill whirled to face him. "You are the only neighbor within two miles."

"What'd I tell you?" He flashed her an insolent grin.

Jill glared at him, refusing to be coaxed into a better humor. Remy reluctantly turned serious once again. "What are your plans?" he probed.

Jill was silent. She picked up a pen and clenched it tightly, her expression worried. "I don't know," she admitted reluctantly. "I haven't talked to Aunt Hildy yet, because I didn't want to upset her after she had just been admitted to the hospital, but when the time is right, I'm hoping to talk her into moving back to New York with me."

I should have seen this coming, Remy thought. "New York," he repeated, then shook his head in silent remonstration. *Hildy would never be happy there.*

"My plan makes perfect sense, Mr. Beauregard." Her voice was low, persuasive. "She can't live alone any longer. I miss not seeing her on a daily basis and I know she misses me, as well."

The thought of sweet, seventy-five-year-old Hildy Sutherland being carted around for her niece's convenience made Remy's blood boil. "Oh, your plan makes perfect sense, all right. You're doing all this out of guilt, aren't you?"

Jill blinked. "I beg your pardon?"

He leaned in even closer. She looked as though she was about to run. Not ready to let her go until he'd had his say, he took her by the shoulders. "You weren't here when she fell," Remy continued, "so now you feel like you have to make it up to her by taking complete charge of her life. Never mind what might be best for Hildy!"

Jill tried to wiggle free of his grasp. Remy refused to let her. "I don't have to take this!" she said.

"No, you don't," Remy said, wishing she didn't feel so soft and lithe and womanly beneath his hands.

Abruptly, he released her. "You could fire my Cajun butt—"

Jill glared at him. "I haven't *hired* you yet!"

"And tell me to get outta town, or at least off your property," Remy continued, ignoring the way Jill's breasts rose and lowered with each breath she took. "'Course, that would upset your aunt," Remy drawled as he looked down into Jill's turbulent blue eyes. "Hildy's already been through hell, what with falling and being stranded here for near on an hour, alone, with a badly sprained ankle and a broken arm. Who knows what would have happened if I hadn't noticed her upstairs lights flickering on and off and came by to check up on her."

"I'm perfectly aware how much we owe you, Mr. Beauregard," Jill said stiffly.

"But you don't like owing anybody anything, do you, Jill?"

"No, I don't," she snapped, her cheeks flushing all the more, "and that goes double for low country rogues like you!"

He lifted his brows, amused. "You think I'm a scoundrel, huh?" he chided.

Jill's pretty lips thinned. "I think you'd stop at nothing to get your way, yes."

He hooked his thumbs through the belt loops of his jeans and regarded her with a cocky grin. "Sometimes, yeah, I reckon you're right. Sometimes I see something I've just gotta have and I run right after it and I don't let up until I have it." He looped a strand of her hair around his index finger. It felt just as he thought it would: full, soft and silky.

Jill pushed his hand away. "Well, not this time, buster."

Remy folded his arms in front of him. "Now that we've finished slinging insults at one another, sugar, when do you want me to start with the rewiring?"

Jill glared back at him. She tossed her head. Silky mahogany hair flew in all directions, then settled around her face. "I think a more appropriate question is, 'How soon can you be finished?'"

"HE'S TERRIBLE, Aunt Hildy." Jill began her litany of complaints almost the moment she arrived at the hospital in nearby Baton Rouge, where her great-aunt had been taken shortly after her fall.

"Ornery, you mean, and he is that, all right." Hildy chuckled from her hospital bed. "A real scoundrel."

"You say that as if it's something to be proud of," Jill accused, as she reached behind Hildy to fluff her pillows.

She was relieved her aunt was looking much better today. Her youthful vitality was back and there was color in her face. Her white hair had been neatly combed into the tight curls she favored. Her sprained ankle was still wrapped and elevated, of course, and it would be a good six weeks before her left arm came out of the cast, but the rest of her was in fine shape. As soon as Hildy's ankle was fully healed, her doctor had said Hildy could come home. Until then, she had to get around by wheelchair, since crutches were impossible for someone her age.

"Remy's certainly got your fires lit!" Hildy said, laughing.

"My temper, maybe," Jill conceded sourly. She couldn't recall a man who had been more insolent or more infuriating. The only reason she had stood him as long as she had was because she knew how attached her aunt had become to her new neighbor. Too late, Jill had realized that new neighbor spelled trouble with a capital T.

Her aunt sent her a knowing grin. "Doesn't the fact that he can get you riled up so easily tell you something, precious?"

"Yes," Jill retorted flatly. "It tells me we can't stand each other." She paced the private room restlessly, her high heels *clicking* on the glossy linoleum floor. "If we have to spend even one more minute in each other's company, we'll probably kill each other."

Hildy laughed all the harder. "Kill or kiss?"

"Aunt Hildy, please." Jill tightened her hands into fists. "He's rude!"

Hildy looked shocked. And disbelieving. She plastered a hand to her ample chest. "Our Remy?"

"Yes, *our* Remy!"

"I see you've memorized my name right fine," a syrupy male voice drawled from the open doorway.

Jill's heart immediately sped up. Her knees suddenly had a peculiar weakness. There was a nervous flutter in her stomach, even before she turned toward the sound of that low male voice.

"And Jill's right," Remy continued as he sauntered in with an armful of flowers. He bent and kissed Aunt Hildy. "Your niece and I did get off on the wrong foot, Hildy, but I'm planning to fix that." That said, he turned the full impact of his gaze on her.

Jill ignored the brushfires starting every place on her that his gaze touched. The man was a walking advertisement of Cajun sensuality, but that didn't mean she had to be affected. "Too late," Jill said airily.

"It's never too late," Hildy immediately disagreed.

Flushing with embarrassment, Jill turned away from the mischief she saw sparkling in Remy's dark brown eyes. She regarded her great-aunt in exasperation. "I don't think we're ever going to agree on this, Aunt Hildy," she said firmly. "So maybe we just shouldn't discuss it." *Or him.*

"I know just what your darlin' niece means, Hildy. I've always preferred action to talk myself," Remy drawled with a wicked grin. He pulled up a straight-backed chair on Aunt Hildy's other side and turned it around backward. While Jill watched in mild annoyance, he straddled the seat of the chair, hooked one arm over the top and took Aunt Hildy's hand. "So what can I get you? Some of those pralines you like so well?"

Hildy lit up like a child at Christmas. "Oh, Remy, that'd be wonderful!" she said.

I absolutely hate him, Jill thought.

Remy smiled, his six-foot-four body practically oozing charm. "Anything else?"

"How about the latest issue of *Soap Opera Digest?* I want to read all about Jill's soap!"

Jill didn't want Remy ingratiating himself any further. "Aunt Hildy, I can tell you tons more about what's new and happening with 'The Brave and the Beautiful' than a magazine can."

"I know, dear, but I like to see it in print."

Jill brightened as the next thought struck. "I doubt they have it at the hospital gift shop, but Remy probably wouldn't mind driving to the supermarket down the street." Maybe he'd get lost or waylaid by some pretty girl and she would never see him again.

Aunt Hildy shook her head, vetoing Jill's plan to get rid of her bad-boy neighbor. "Tomorrow's plenty soon enough for Remy to bring me my magazine, Jill. Right now, I just want to visit."

Remy gazed at Jill and grinned. "Foiled again," he teased. Her temper under tight control, Jill simply glared at him in withering silence. Remy turned to Hildy. "Jill wants to get rid of me so she can talk you into having someone else do the rewiring on Magnolia Place."

Hildy became immediately upset. "Is this true, honey?"

Jill had never been one to look a gift horse in the mouth, and Remy had given her the opening she sought. "Remy tells me it's going to be a big job," she said.

"Yep," Remy was quick to concur. He regarded Jill with sparkling eyes that promised to show her every sin imaginable, and then some. "It'll take every night and weekend for the next couple of weeks," he finished huskily.

Jill fought the thrill that went through her whenever he looked at her so intently. "I don't think I'm compatible with him, Aunt Hildy." *I don't think I want to be compatible with him. He's too forward, too charming.*

"Nonsense." Aunt Hildy quickly dismissed Jill's complaint. "You two get along fine."

Jill thought about the way Remy looked at her, like some ripe Georgia peach he was just dying to taste. She thought about the way her mouth dried out whenever he was too near. "No, we don't, Aunt Hildy."

"Then you will," Aunt Hildy replied, just as firmly.

Jill could feel Remy's laughter even though he didn't make a sound. Ignoring the triumph sparkling in his sable brown eyes, she persisted sweetly, "But he's awfully busy."

"Never too busy to help you out, Hildy," Remy interjected pleasantly. "You either, Jill."

"Can't we just get someone else? Someone who could work on the project full-time and not just nights and weekends?" Someone who didn't wear bright blue bill caps that said Cajuns Do It All Better, or starched white oxford cloth shirts with the first button undone and the sleeves rolled up to just below his elbows. Someone who didn't wear soft faded jeans that fit like a glove, outlining long, muscled legs and an abundant sex.

"Honey, Remy here is the best electrician in the parish. He is the only one I trust to work on Magnolia Place and not make an infernal mess of things."

He's already made an infernal mess of things, Jill thought. *When he's around, I can't think straight!*

"I'm sure the two of you will get along fine once you get to know each other," Hildy continued. "Now if you don't mind, darlings, I'm feeling a little tired."

"Of course, you need your rest." Jill looked at Remy, silently imploring him to leave. Now. To her surprise, he took the hint.

"I'll be by tomorrow," Remy said, bending to gently kiss the back of Aunt Hildy's hand. "You call me if you need anything."

"I will," Aunt Hildy promised. "And, Remy, thank you, darlin', for being such a good boy. I'll rest easier knowing you're around to keep an eye on my precious Jill."

It was all Jill could do not to roll her eyes at that. If only her dear aunt knew.... Jill had the feeling that given the slightest encouragement, the slightest permission, Remy would have her in bed in two seconds flat. Fortunately, Jill was too smart and too cautious to have affairs. No, she was holding out for the real thing, not just some hot, wild toss in the hay with a Louisiana bad boy.

"It's my pleasure, Hildy." Remy looked at Jill. "It was good to see you again, Miss Jill," he said humbly.

I only wish I could say the same, Jill thought, but in deference to her aunt's presence, Jill held her tongue. Her aunt had brought her up to be a lady. Ladies were calm and courteous at all times. Ladies did not sink to the level of someone like Remy Beauregard. "Meeting you was indeed an occasion, Mr. Beauregard," Jill said with stiff formality. *And not a good one!*

In an effort to hasten his departure, she rose and walked him as far as the door. He paused in the portal and looked down at her, towering over her a good five or six inches. Jill thought about the way Remy had looked her over that afternoon, with slow hungry deliberation, and the hot mischievous look in his eyes said he was thinking the same. The flush of embarrassment warmed her cheeks. She knew he found her attractive. What she didn't understand was why she found him attractive, when she knew he was no good for her. She was usually more sensible.

"You needn't bother with the magazine or the pralines," Jill told Remy. "I'll pick them up for my aunt tomorrow."

"Oh, it's no trouble," Remy said. The look in his eyes said he wasn't letting her off the hook that easily.

Jill dished it right back. "And now that I'm here, there's also no need for you to be dropping by the hospital so often."

Remy folded his sinewy arms across his broad chest. "Also no trouble," Remy replied.

"Yes, Remy, do come visit. You know how I love hearing your tall tales!" Hildy encouraged drowsily from her hospital bed.

Jill put her hand on Remy's shoulder and practically shoved him out the door. "Thank you for stopping by, Mr. Beauregard," she said loudly.

"With two such lovely ladies, the pleasure was all mine," Remy drawled. He stuck his head back in the door, smiled at Hildy and waved goodbye.

Hildy chuckled. "Scoundrel," she murmured approvingly. "Through and through!"

"Amen to that," Jill muttered under her breath, so only Remy could hear. And unlike her aunt, she didn't consider it a virtue.

Remy chucked her under the chin. His hot gaze roved her slowly from head to toe. "I'll be seeing you, sugar."

Jill glared at him. "Not if I have anything to do with it," she said.

Chapter Two

"What the heck...?" Jill stopped just inside the Magnolia Place kitchen and stared at the eight clotheslines strung back and forth across the large century-old room. She didn't know what was going on here, but she had a bad feeling about this.

Kizzie Lafitte, her aunt's eccentric part-time housekeeper, emerged from the adjacent laundry room with a laundry basket of damp linen balanced on her thin hip. As usual, Kizzie was dressed in a tattered bill cap, a faded floral housedress, sparkling white socks and spit-polished black combat boots.

Calmly, Kizzie began draping wet sheets over the clotheslines she had strung from cabinet door to cabinet door.

Jill sighed. It was late, nearly 10:00 p.m. She had already made two visits to the hospital to see her aunt, and had two run-ins with Remy Beauregard. She really didn't want to deal with this, too. But it looked as if she didn't have any choice. Kizzie had apparently thrown down the gauntlet. "Kizzie, what are you doing?" Jill asked wearily.

"What does it look like I'm doing?" Kizzie asked grumpily. "I'm drying the bed sheets and pillow-cases."

Jill admired hard work and dedication. Deliberate inefficiency was another matter. She frowned. "Is the dryer not working?"

Kizzie shrugged carelessly. "Last I checked, the dryer was working fine," she said bluntly.

"Then why aren't you using it to dry the sheets?"

Kizzie looked at Jill as if Jill were out of her mind. "Because we always dry the sheets on the line. Miz Hildy likes them stiff and starchy. The dryer makes them soft."

Jill's stomach rumbled hungrily but she couldn't get to the refrigerator or the pantry because the lines of sheets and pillowcases were in the way. "Do you always dry them in the kitchen?"

"When I wash them after the sun goes down, I do."

Jill's stomach growled again, reminding her that it had literally been hours since she'd eaten. "Look, this once, couldn't we just put the bed linens in the dryer?" Jill said.

Kizzie's sunburned jaw set stubbornly. "Miz Hildy lets me do things my way."

"I know, Kizzie," Jill said gently. "But Miss Hildy isn't here right now, and I would prefer it if you dried the sheets in the dryer and came in to do your work during the day."

"Miz Hildy lets me come in whenever I want, night or day or both if I want," Kizzie retorted belliger-ently.

"I'd still prefer it if we could set regular hours."

"I don't like regular hours," Kizzie stated.

"Okay, then we'll take it day by day. I just need to know *when* to expect you."

"I don't know *when* you should expect me. I just come in whenever I feel like it, and if I don't feel like it then I don't come in. That system always worked fine for Miz Hildy and me."

Jill rubbed the back of her neck and wished she weren't so exhausted. "I doubt most employers would be as generous as my aunt, Kizzie."

"I ain't working for most employers. I'm working for Hildy." Kizzie paused. She turned a strand of wiry faded brown hair beneath her tattered Billy's Tavern cap, then tugged the brim a little farther down her neck. "Aren't I?"

"Well, yes." Jill folded her arms in front of her and leaned against the doorframe. "The thing is, Kizzie, I need a lot of peace and quiet to get my work done. If you could just tell me when you'll be here, and what you're going to be doing while you're here, then I'll try to work around you so we don't get in each other's way. Okay?"

Without a word, Kizzie flung off her apron, snatched up her lunch pail and stomped out the door.

"Kizzie?" Jill followed her as far as the back porch. Kizzie didn't turn around. "Kizzie, come back here, please!" Jill wasn't about to go chasing after Kizzie in the blackness of night.

"Got a real way with people, don't you?"

The sound of that syrupy drawl sent shivers down Jill's spine. She marched back into the kitchen, or at least as far into one corner of it as she could get. Remy lounged in the portal. Jill put her hands on her hips. Hot color flowed in her cheeks. "What are you doing here?" she demanded.

Half his mouth crooked up in a tantalizing smile. "I told you I could only work nights and weekends," he reminded in a low voice that dripped sensuality.

Jill blew out an exasperated breath. So much for her wish that she not have to deal with Remy again today. "Well, it's late," she said.

Remy inclined his head in the direction of the back door. "What'd you say to Kizzie, anyway? I've never seen her so ticked off."

"I suggested she dry her sheets in the dryer."

"Not smart, sugar. What else?"

"I merely suggested that we establish some sort of regular working hours for her while I'm here."

"Bet that went over like a lead balloon."

Jill hated being put on the defensive. "It is not an unreasonable request," she informed him archly.

"Maybe not to a clock puncher like you," Remy agreed, his sable eyes serious. "But to a swamp person like Kizzie..." He left the thought unfinished.

"Look, Remy, doing things to your employer's satisfaction is what having a job is all about."

Remy looked Jill over skeptically. "Hildy was always satisfied with whatever Kizzie did. In fact, she said there wasn't another woman on earth who could make a place shine the way Kizzie does."

A fresh wave of guilt rushed through Jill. "I know that."

"Then you also know Kizzie has worked for your great-aunt for nigh on six years now and never once let her down," Remy said gently.

That wasn't quite true, Jill thought. "Except the night Aunt Hildy fell," Jill said.

Remy's head lifted. His dark eyes sparkled with recognition. "Ah, so that's it. You blame her for not being here to call the ambulance right away."

Jill's gaze clashed with Remy's. "I blame her for refusing to work regular hours, like every other normal person."

"Kizzie's not normal, at least not your definition of city-slick normal." Remy pushed a sheet aside impatiently, ducked beneath a clothesline and stepped closer to Jill. His voice dropped to a confiding murmur. "I thought you knew that. She was born and raised in the swamp. She's lived there all her life. Only reason she came out to work for Miss Hildy was to help put her kids through school, 'cause *they* didn't want to live all *their* lives in the swamp."

Jill lifted the sheet closest to her off the line and dumped it into the basket Kizzie had left on the kitchen floor. "I didn't know that."

Remy helped Jill take another sheet off the line. And then the next and the next. Soon, they had taken them all down again. Jill carried them into the adjacent laundry room, tossed them in the dryer and switched it on.

"I'll apologize to her tomorrow," Jill continued.

Remy cast her a doubtful look as they both returned to the kitchen. "Good luck."

Without warning, the kitchen lights began to flicker. The clothes dryer lurched to a noisy halt. Jill turned to Remy in exasperation. It seemed every time he was around, chaos reigned. He had to be at fault—either inadvertently, because he was just pure bad luck, or deliberately, because he was playing games with her. "Now what did you do?" she demanded.

"Nothing yet, at least not in here," Remy replied amiably, his eyes warming to hers. "I just carried in the coils of new wire I bought after I left the hospital and left them upstairs in one of the bedrooms." He paused, then began taking the clotheslines down, too. "That's okay, isn't it?"

"Sure. I guess." Jill looked around at the lights, which were still flickering on and off rather eerily. It couldn't be the dryer causing the problem—it was no longer running and the lights were still malfunctioning. "Then what's with the lights?" she asked. Magnolia Place was a glorious old home when everything was working properly. When they weren't, it could be a little spooky.

Remy shrugged. "Could be Kizzie," he speculated.

Jill blinked. "Kizzie's been messing with the wiring?" Her stomach growled again, reminding her how hungry she was.

"No, of course not."

Another series of flickering ensued, even longer than the others. A chill coursed down Jill's spine. She resisted the urge to step closer to Remy and take shelter against his tall, strong body. She went to the refrigerator instead, opened the door and pulled out a platter of baked ham. "Then why did you say that?"

Remy started to speak, then stopped. "Never mind."

Jill kept the refrigerator open with one hip. To her relief, the lights had suddenly stopped flickering again. She reached in and brought out the bread, lettuce and jars of mustard and pickles. "What do you mean, 'Never mind'?" she persisted bad-temperedly. "Why did you say that?" She hated it when anyone left her hanging.

Deciding she needed some coffee, too, she went to the coffeemaker on the counter and, realizing the flow of electric power in the house had stabilized once again, set about quickly making a fresh pot. Remy followed her, looking as if he had all the time in the world to stand around and chat with her. Considering the rather laid-back schedule he kept, maybe he did.

"Well, as I was saying before, Kizzie's lived all her life in the swamp, you know, and she wasn't exactly happy with you when she left just a second ago."

Jill looked up at Remy. He was standing very close to her. All at once, she noticed several things. He looked as if he had shaved since he'd been at the hospital. He wasn't wearing his obnoxious bill cap any longer, either. His sandy hair was cut in long, wind-swept layers that curled across his forehead, the tops of his ears and down the back of his neck in sexy disarray. It looked touchable, soft and clean.

She shouldn't be thinking about things like this! So the man had nice hair. So he was very good-looking in a roguish sort of way. So what?

"So what does Kizzie living in the swamp all her life have to do with my lights flickering off and on?" Jill asked impatiently. Finished making the coffee, she switched it on and went back to the business of assembling a sandwich.

Remy rubbed at the back of his neck, offered a sheepish grin and entirely avoided Jill's eyes. "She's a little into Cajun folk magic," he said.

Jill stopped trying to wrestle with the bread wrapper and simply looked at him. "Cajun folk magic?" she repeated.

"Yeah." Remy straightened against the counter. His expression became abruptly, facetiously serious. "It's a way of controlling life or exerting influence using a combination of popular folklore, herbs and potions and superstitious beliefs. Folk medicine and old wives' tales are both offshoots of it."

Jill rolled her eyes. She went back to the dryer and as a test, switched it on. To her relief, it resumed normal operation. "I grew up in Louisiana, Remy," she said. Satisfied all was well, she returned to the kitchen. "I know what Cajun folk magic is. I just can't believe that—" she crossed the distance between them swiftly and planted the tip of her index finger on the middle of his chest "—*you're* actually standing there trying to scare me with such a thing."

Remy caught her hand and cupped it against his chest. "Not scare," he corrected as his fingers closed around hers in a warm, protective manner. "Warn. Kizzie is no woman to cross."

Where her palm rested against his chest, Jill could feel the steady thrumming of his heart. Even more disturbing was the information that Remy's chest was every bit as solid and strong as it looked beneath the starched white oxford cloth shirt. "Well, just so you'll know," Jill said, yanking her hand from his, "I don't believe in Cajun folk magic." Noticing the coffee had stopped brewing, she took the filter off, snapped the serving cap into place and poured herself a mug.

Remy reached for a mug, too. "That's not a very wise attitude to have around Kizzie," he said as he filled his mug.

Jill carried her coffee over to the sandwich fixings and set it down on the counter beside them. "Now I suppose you're telling me you believe in Cajun folk magic, too," she said, making no effort to keep the sarcasm from her voice.

Remy rested his mug against his chest, in the exact same place where her hand had just been. His dark brown eyes stayed fixed on hers. "I believe in what it can do," he admitted with a faint smile.

Jill got out the powdered creamer for her coffee and unscrewed the lid. "And what, pray tell, can Cajun folk magic do?" she prodded, tongue-in-cheek.

Remy took a long sip of his coffee, his glittering eyes never leaving her face. "It can excite people, tap into their innate superstitious beliefs and really stir things up," he said.

Jill shook her head as she began assembling her sandwich. "You must really think I'm a moron to believe the lights were flickering on and off because of some Cajun folk magic spell Kizzie put on the kitchen!"

"You two were arguing just before it happened," Remy pointed out, watching as Jill slapped two pieces of bread on a plate and followed it with a slice of ham and two pieces of lettuce. "Seconds after she storms out the lights go off. Coincidence?" Remy dipped his head in mock censure and teased, "I think not."

Jill unscrewed the lid on the jar of mustard. She slathered some on her sandwich, then realized she still hadn't added creamer to her coffee and the brew was cooling fast. She reached for the spoon. "It was, too, a coincidence." She looked up at his face as she spoke.

Remy grinned and held her eyes. "Like I said," he drawled, his eyes tracking the new warmth in her cheeks, "Cajun folk magic brings excitement. In your case, lots of it," he said as Jill added a large spoonful of powdered creamer to her coffee.

Jill blew out an exasperated breath and shook her head. "I may be out of patience with you, Mr. Beauregard, but I am not excited," she said, as she continued stirring her coffee.

"Oh, I can see that." Remy chuckled.

Jill looked down in the direction of his gaze, and saw she had just stirred a generous dollop of Dijon mustard into her coffee. He was laughing at her, thinking she had made such a mistake because she was upset about the possibility of Kizzie using Cajun folk magic on her. Jill knew better. It wasn't Cajun folk magic unnerving her. It was Remy, standing so close, looking so good and sexy and relaxed. So very male.

Half his mouth crooked up into a generous smile. "You always drink your coffee that way?" He seemed to be daring her to make the claim.

"Sure," Jill said, not about to let him emerge the victor here or at any other time. "It's a Yankee tradition. You know how crazy we New Yorkers are."

Remy's grin broadened. "I don't believe you, sugar," he said softly.

His words were like a double dare, and Jill never refused one of those. She lifted her mug to her lips and took a sip of the bayou brown liquid. The combination of Dijon mustard and New Orleans-style chicory coffee was so bad, her eyes watered. But Jill forced herself to swallow, and then smile as if she'd just tasted the most delicious delicacy she'd ever enjoyed in her life. She fibbed with as much satisfaction as she could muster. "There, just the way I like it."

"Uh-huh. If you don't mind, I think I'll pass on that particular New York delicacy," Remy drawled.

"Whatever," Jill said with a shrug. She went back to finishing up her sandwich with more than her usual care.

"You know, if you were a lady, you'd offer me one of those, too," Remy said.

"Where you're concerned, I'm no lady, Remy Beauregard," Jill grumbled bad-temperedly, and saw his eyes light up even more. Then she thought about him passing this lapse in her manners on to Hildy, who would be aghast. "But help yourself anyway," Jill said grudgingly.

"Thanks." Remy quickly made himself a sandwich, then joined her at the kitchen table. As he sat across from her, his glance was glimmering with mischief. "So is it okay if I start working on the parlor tonight?"

"Actually, it would be nice if you could just get in there and do it and get out, since that's the room I've been using as my office."

"Okay," Remy said amiably. "I think I can manage to do it all tonight."

"Okay?" Jill echoed, surprised. "Just like that?" She wondered uneasily what the catch was. Thus far, he hadn't done anything she wanted him to do.

The dimples around Remy's sensuous mouth deepened. "You expect me to argue with you, sugar?"

Jill shrugged and regarded him with caution. "You have about everything else," she reminded slowly.

His eyes took a lazy, thorough tour of her person. "You'll find I can be a very cooperative man," he drawled. "When I want to be."

Jill refused to dignify his teasing with a similar response. "I trust you'll be out of here by midnight," she said coolly, knowing even if he left right this second it wouldn't be soon enough for her.

Remy spread his hands wide. "Who knows? It takes as long as it takes."

That was what she got for allowing her aunt to insist they allow the laid-back Southern charmer to do the work. Didn't Jill know, from past bitter experience, to be wary of men who looked like a dream and made promises as easily as they drew breath? Promises they often had no intention of keeping! "Well, be out of here by midnight, anyway," Jill ordered decisively. She took what was left of her sandwich and stormed off. The only way she would be able to enjoy her meal was if he wasn't around.

"You forgot your coffee, sugar," Remy said.

Jill ignored him. His lazy laughter followed her down the hall and up the stairs. To Jill's burning ears, it sounded like a taunting precursor of things to come.

"HERE YOU GO, SUGAR."

Jill woke to the delicious smells of fresh chicory coffee and piping hot beignets. Sleep still clouding her brain, she struggled to sit up as Remy Beauregard handed her a plate. Her first coherent thought was, *He shouldn't be here.* Her second thought was, *But of course he is.* She had to do something about the key he had to the house. In the meantime, she'd just bluff her way through the latest catastrophe waiting to happen. There was no reason he had to know how upsetting she found his presence in her bedroom first thing in the morning. It would be enough to make damn sure it never happened again.

"Where'd you get beignets this time of morning?" Jill yawned.

"I made 'em, sugar."

Jill eyed the square, New Orleans-style doughnuts. They were fried to golden brown perfection, dusted liberally with confectioner's sugar and even to her extremely critical eye, looked expertly made.

"I figured it was only fair that I feed you breakfast, since you fed me a sandwich and coffee last night. Besides, I owe you a welcome to the neighborhood," Remy continued as he poured her a cup of coffee. He picked up a jar of Dijon mustard, unscrewed the lid and, with a great show of obsequiousness, scooped up a large spoonful. "Hang on a second and I'll have your coffee for you, too, just the way you like it," he promised.

Jill had barely been able to get down a swallow of the mustard-laced coffee the evening before; she knew she'd never manage it first thing in the morning, even to save her pride. Swiftly she lifted her hand to stop him. "I only use mustard in my evening coffee," she fibbed. "I use cream in the morning, Remy."

Remy gave her a knowing smile. "Well, what do you know, there was a container of that down in the fridge, and I just happened to bring it up with me."

Their hands touched as he handed her the carton of cream and despite her attempt to hate him as much as she hated his postdawn intrusion, Jill couldn't help but notice how good he looked. He hadn't had much more sleep than she'd had, which amounted to about five hours, but he looked fresh as a daisy. He smelled of shampoo and soap.

Remy watched her pour cream in her coffee. "Hmm. Cream in the morning, mustard at night. I'll be sure and remember that," he teased.

Jill was sure he would. She sipped her coffee in silence, trying to figure out how to handle this. Aunt Hildy obviously looked on Remy more as the son she'd never had than as a neighbor. But that didn't mean Jill had to feel the same.

Feeling a little more awake after several sips of the strong chicory coffee, Jill asked, "What are you really doing here, Remy?" Did he really think he could score points with her this way? And what did he really want from her and her aunt? Part of Hildy's inheritance? What? He had to have some angle; men like Remy always did.

Remy had been pacing back and forth before the windows. He stopped and turned to face her, his dark brown eyes meeting hers in a sparkling show of sincerity. "I promised Hildy I'd keep an eye on you while you were around. And I wanted you to know I called the hospital first thing. Hildy had a restful night and the nurse said the swelling on her ankle seems to have gone down, just a little. They're going to let her sit in a wheelchair for a while today." He shrugged, as if acts of gallantry were commonplace for him. "I thought you'd want to know."

Jill was impressed by his thoughtfulness in dropping by, even if she didn't appreciate his presumptuousness in coming up to her bedroom uninvited. "Thanks." She sipped her coffee some more, then set the mug on the doily-covered nightstand beside her bed. "But you can't just stop by anytime you like and walk into my bedroom."

Remy grinned and sauntered closer. The look of choirboy innocence on his face told Jill she was in no imminent danger. "Why not?" he asked guilelessly.

Jill gave him a look that spoke volumes. "Because it's not proper."

"What's not proper?" Remy slapped a hand across his chest. "I'm dressed. And you're…half-dressed."

Jill glanced down. The U-shaped bodice on her white lawn gown dipped precariously low over one breast. She hurriedly straightened it. "You know what I mean," she said irritably, determined not to let him get to her, no matter how much he tried.

"No, I'm not sure I do." He waited, his gaze flirtatious.

"If someone found out you were in my bedroom first thing in the morning, they'd think—"

Remy sat on the bed beside her, his expression perplexed. "What?" He seemed to be daring her to go on.

Jill clasped the covers to her collarbone and plunged on determinedly. "That we were . . . you know."

"What?" Remy asked.

"Fooling around!"

Remy leaned over her. He planted a hand on either side of her, trapping her back against the pillows. "Like this?" The next thing Jill knew, his mouth had come down on hers. His lips were soft and sensuous as they molded to hers. And though she knew she should fight, she seemed suddenly to have lost her will. Her limbs were heavy, and her body was throbbing with an odd, disturbing ache.

As their world narrowed even more, to just the two of them, she felt light-headed to the point of being disoriented, and yet she was strangely unable to fight it. Maybe because this whole scene was like some fantasy romance she had penned for "The Brave and the Beautiful." Only, this wasn't a soap, Jill reminded herself sternly as Remy Beauregard's lips continued to caress hers with disturbing softness, it was real life. And there was no room in her real life for such nonsense. Her normal good sense regained, Jill inhaled jerkily, pressed a hand to Remy's chest and shoved with all her might. "Remy Beauregard," she stormed, "you get out of my bedroom this instant!"

Remy sat back but made no effort to get off the bed. "Sure now?" he teased softly with an unrepentant grin. "Myself, I could go for another kiss."

In answer, Jill did the unthinkable. She picked up her half-filled mug of coffee off the nightstand and hurled it at him. Coffee sprayed his shirt and jeans and splashed up into his face, ruining his just-shaved and -showered morning freshness.

She expected him to be furious with her. Instead, he was pleased. His laughter erupted in the morning silence of her bedroom. "Ooh la la, you're fiery in the morning, sugar." Remy chuckled as he rolled lazily to his feet. Coffee dripped down his nose and onto his shirt; yet he seemed delighted with her unprecedentedly passionate response, both during and after his kiss.

Jill didn't know quite what it was about this man that got to her so much, but she knew that she had had enough. She flung back the covers, stood on top of the bed and pointed to the door. "Out!" she snapped. "Right now!"

Remy tilted his head and surveyed her legs with unabashed interest. "Guess that means you want me to leave, huh?"

Jill tossed a pillow at him, then another and another. Laughing, he caught them all and held them to his chest. "This an invitation for a pillow fight, sugar?" he drawled as he swaggered another foot closer, until his long legs touched the side of the bed once again.

"No." Jill dashed off the bed and across the room to get her robe.

Leaning against the foot of her bed, Remy watched her shrug on the silk wrapper. He cocked a sandy brow. "Sure about that now?" he teased.

Jill yanked open her bedroom door. "Dead sure."

"Maybe some other time then." Still laughing, Remy sauntered toward her and dropped the bed pillows one by one at her feet. "I've got a job for a paying customer today but I'll be back later to continue work on the rewiring here," he promised. His eyes roved her lazily, taking in her mussed hair and her flushed cheeks. "What are you going to do?"

Something that should have been done a very long time ago, Jill thought. "Wouldn't you like to know."

Chapter Three

"Are you okay, boss? You sound stressed," Jill's New York assistant, Patty Morgan, said.

"I *am* stressed," Jill said emphatically as she held the portable phone closer to her ear. She had only been back in Louisiana thirty-six hours, and already she was strung tighter than piano wire.

"What's all that racket?"

Jill blocked out the whine of a power drill with the palm of her hand. "The locksmith is here changing the locks."

"Why?"

"Personal protection," she said dryly. She strode into the dining room where she could talk without having to shout to be heard and looked out the bay window, at the blooming azaleas that surrounded Magnolia Place. "I've got a sexy hunk of an electrician living next door who seems to think I've got nothing better to do with my time than get romantically involved."

Patty chuckled. "And you're complaining?"

"Wait, there's more," Jill quipped, tongue-in-cheek. "The electrical problems that caused my aunt's fall extend to the whole house."

"Don't tell me," Jill's assistant guessed breathlessly, "the sexy hunk agreed to fix them."

"And for free," Jill emphasized wryly.

"Well, that sounds nice," Patty said.

Jill shook her head. "Too nice. I think there's a catch, and I may be it." Jill pressed her lips together tightly and tried not to think about the soft, shattering sensuality of Remy Beauregard's kiss. He hadn't even put his tongue inside her mouth and yet his kiss had been more deeply intimate, more frankly arousing, than any other she'd ever received. Just thinking about what he had done to her, the way he'd made her feel, made her tremble with outrage.

"What do you mean you're the catch?" Patty said.

"I mean, I think he expects me to allow him to seduce me as payment for rewiring Magnolia Place!" Jill explained irritably.

Patty laughed. "The guy's clueless, right?"

"You got it." Jill wasn't about to have a fling, now or at any other time or in any other place. She wanted enduring love that would last a lifetime and withstand the pressures of a two-career marriage. If she couldn't have that, then she wouldn't have anything, thank you very much.

"Have you talked to your aunt yet about relocating to New York?"

Jill cupped the phone closer to her ear and tried not to let the worry she felt overwhelm her. "I'm working up to it."

"I know how close the two of you are," Patty said gently. "I'm sure she'll jump at the chance to be closer to you."

"Maybe, if it weren't for Kizzie and Remy and all the ladies in her garden club. . . ." Jill said.

"Who's Kizzie?" Patty asked.

"My great-aunt's housekeeper."

"And Remy?"

"The sexy hunk next door."

"Ah, so he's charming your aunt, too," Patty surmised wisely.

"He's charmed Hildy," Jill corrected quickly. "Not me." Nor would he ever, she determined firmly. She knew men like Remy. Their coaxing smiles usually covered very secret, very self-serving agendas.

"Well, sounds like everything is under control, then," Patty said with relief. "And that's good, because things are *not* under control here."

"Why?" Jill felt her shoulders tense even more. These last few days, she had never felt more torn between her work and her family. "What's going on?"

"The staff writers are in an argument on how to handle the breakup scene between Felicity and Beau. So far, we have three different versions, and after six hours of wrangling yesterday, still no consensus."

Jill picked up a pen and began to make notes on the legal pad in front of her. "Fax me the pages and I'll take a look at them."

"I was hoping you'd say that," Patty said.

"What else?"

"We're behind on the scripts for the next sweeps period."

Jill checked her watch and kept writing. "Set up a conference call with the writers for noon."

"Got it. And sorry to pressure you, but the network brass want to see the bible for next year ASAP. How's it coming?"

"Not as quickly as I had hoped," Jill admitted with a sigh as she tucked a pencil behind her ear. "I've had a lot of distractions." Most of them involving Remy or Hildy or both.

"Want me to stall the brass?"

"Please," Jill said, then looked up to see Kizzie standing in the doorway. She had a bucket in one hand, a scrub brush in the other and a militant-as-hell expression on her face. It looked like this couldn't wait, either, Jill thought. "Listen, I've got to go." Jill concluded her business with her assistant and hung up the phone. She had been thinking about this all morning, and half the afternoon, and she knew what she had to do to make things right. "Kizzie, about last night…" she began congenially. "I'm sorry we got off on the wrong foot."

Kizzie remained where she was and faced Jill in stubborn silence. Beside Jill, the fax began to spit out pages, one after another.

"I'm really glad you're here today," Jill tried again. "I think it's important we straighten things out."

Kizzie cast Jill a doubtful look. She picked up the bucket, turned her back to Jill and got down on her hands and knees and began to scrub the parquet floor.

Jill got the message. Nothing was going to be resolved between the two of them until Kizzie was good and ready. And Kizzie wasn't ready. Sighing, Jill picked up her yellow notepad, several pens and the newly faxed script pages. She might as well get started on her work now, and to get started, she needed a fresh pot of coffee.

She headed for the kitchen and once again stopped just inside the portal. The sheets and pillowcases she'd taken down the night before and dried in the dryer were now soaking wet and hanging up again. As usual, Kizzie had had the last word.

"MY QUESTION IS, Dr. Destrehan, how soon will my aunt be able to travel?" Jill asked, not at all bothered that her aunt's thirty-something physician looked and dressed more like a husband-hunting Southern belle than a health-care professional. Carole Destrehan had come highly recommended, and her aunt liked her. That was all that mattered.

"That depends on what you mean by 'travel,'" Carole Destrehan said as she sank into one of the straight-backed embroidered chairs in Hildy's parlor and smoothed the skirt of her tea-length floral dress over her knees.

Jill poured tea from the silver service. "I want to take Hildy back to New York with me, providing I can convince her to go."

Carole balanced her saucer and cup on her lap, and took one of the cucumber-and-cream-cheese sandwiches Jill offered. "You haven't talked to Hildy about it yet?"

"I've been working up to it," Jill confessed on a worried sigh as the fax machine on the other side of the room spit out another series of work-related papers. "The problem is, I didn't know what kind of physical therapy, if any, was going to be involved in her recovery. That's why I asked if I could talk to you privately this afternoon," Jill finished. It had been Carole's idea to stop by Magnolia Place after office hours on her way home.

"I don't anticipate Hildy needing any rehabilitative therapy for her broken arm, but we won't know for sure until we take the cast off in six weeks. Her release from the hospital, however, will depend primarily on her ankle," Carole said. "As you know, her sprain is a mild one. The swelling has already started to go down and may be gone altogether in another day or two, but she is still having pain, and as long as she has pain, I want her off that ankle. Period. Until she can walk comfortably again, I won't be releasing her from the hospital in Baton Rouge."

"So in other words, it'll be at least another week before Aunt Hildy will be released?" Jill asked, trying hard to mask her disappointment.

"As close as I can figure, yes," Carole said, sweeping her hand through her shoulder-length honey blond hair. "But there's something else you should be aware of, Jill. Older people often don't do well after a change in environment. Just moving an older person from their home into a smaller apartment in the same area can be traumatic for them. You're talking about a major change, one that shouldn't be undertaken lightly."

Jill wanted to do what was best for her aunt. She also wanted Hildy close by during her recuperation.

"Aunt Hildy's always loved New York whenever she's come to see me there."

"Visiting somewhere is different from actually living there," Carole pointed out gently. "You really need to think about this, Jill. Above all, don't push your aunt into anything, particularly so soon after her accident. Give Hildy time to think things through. It may be that just hiring live-in help for the next few months will be enough to ensure your aunt's full recovery, without disrupting her life or taking her away from her friends and her independence altogether."

Carole's sage advice struck a nerve. Jill knew what happened to Hildy could happen to anyone, young or old. Nevertheless, Jill still felt very bad about not being there to rescue her aunt from her fall, and she worried about the same thing happening again. Darn it all, Jill hated living so far from her aunt, just as she hated the idea of Hildy having to recuperate from her injury without Jill being there to administer daily doses of tender loving care and make sure everything went smoothly. Hildy had cared for Jill for much of Jill's young life. It was Jill's turn to care for Hildy now. But how?

Remy strolled in, his tool belt jangling around his slim waist. Seeing him, Carole lit up like a wallflower who'd just been asked to dance. Jill felt a flash of jealousy. Telling herself she was behaving like an idiot—she had no claim on Remy Beauregard, after all—she firmly pushed the feeling away.

"Hi, darlin'." Remy bent and kissed the femininely dressed physician on the cheek. "I haven't seen you since I fixed that short in your office."

Carole returned the casual kiss and then stood. "I've been around." She patted him on the arm. Jill couldn't decide whether it was a friendly pat, or an I-want-to-get-to-know-you-better kind of pat. Her green eyes sparkling, Carole smiled back at Remy warmly. "Call me sometime. We'll go to dinner again. Or better yet, we'll drive into New Orleans and have beignets and chicory coffee in the Café du Monde."

Again? Did Remy come on to all the women whose homes and offices he worked in? Had he kissed Carole the way he had kissed her? Brought Carole coffee and beignets in the morning, not in her bedroom, but at her desk at the office?

Oblivious to the jealous nature of Jill's thoughts, Remy gave Carole a bluntly inquiring look. "You here to help Jill figure out how to move her aunt to New York City?" he chided with frank disapproval.

"This is Jill's dilemma, Remy. I suggest you let her handle it as she sees best," Carole reprimanded lightly. She handed Jill her business card with a number scrawled on the back. "I've got the names of several excellent companions, all of whom live in on-contractual basis. Call me if you decide you want to start interviewing them for your aunt. I've also got physician friends in the New York area who could be of similar help in referring you to people there."

"Thanks," Jill said. Though how she was going to get her aunt to agree to a full-time companion, even for a few months, was anyone's guess. Hildy had always been independent to a fault.

Remy turned to Jill as soon as Carole had left. His expression was grim and disapproving. "Talking Hildy into something to her face is one thing," he said. "Going behind her back to make arrangements without even consulting her is something else entirely."

Jill sighed, not sure why she was bothering to defend herself to him. "I wasn't—"

"Yeah?" He quirked a disbelieving brow. "Does Hildy know you just met with Carole? And since this was about Hildy, why wasn't the meeting held in the hospital with Hildy present?"

"Because I didn't want to upset her."

"Telling her later how you've been going behind her back now won't manage that?" Remy said with a scowl. Without waiting for her reply, he turned on his heel and left the house. Sensing he was about to do something *she* would regret, Jill rushed after Remy, finally catching up with him at the bottom of the steps leading up to the raised cottage-style plantation home. "Remy, where are you going?"

Remy strode past the blooming azaleas. "To the hospital, to see your aunt." He looked her straight in the eye. "Someone needs to tell her what you've been up to before it's too late for her to let you know how she really feels on this subject."

"I do know," Jill insisted.

Again, he looked as if he didn't buy in to that. "If that's the truth, then why are you meeting with her doctor behind her back and making plans to move her to New York?"

Jill had no ready answer for that, at least none that Remy Beauregard would buy. His mouth grim, Remy climbed in his pickup, gunned the motor and took off.

Jill swore. Damn that Remy. Now she had no choice
but to go back inside, get her car keys and follow him
to the hospital in Baton Rouge.

By the time she reached her aunt's private room on
the second floor some twenty-five minutes later, Remy
was already at her Aunt Hildy's bedside. From the
troubled looks on both their faces, Jill guessed Remy
had already filled her aunt in on Jill's meeting with
Carole.

Jill put her purse down and crossed to her aunt's
side. She was furious with Remy for having broken the
news to Hildy this way, but knew she had to stay calm
for Hildy's sake. "I guess Remy told you I had your
doctor out to the house for a private talk," Jill began
reluctantly.

Hildy's cheeks were pink with indignation but her
manner was calm. "Yes, he did, and, honey, as much
as I appreciate your concern, I really do not want to
move to New York or hire a companion."

Jill studied her aunt who, like herself, had an over-
abundance of stiff-necked pride. "Aunt Hildy, you
know I don't want to pressure you into anything, but
like it or not, we have to face the facts," Jill said
gently. She clasped Hildy's soft hand, all too aware of
how much frailer it felt this visit when compared to the
last. "You can't continue to live alone as long as your
arm is in a cast, and you are still nursing a sprained
ankle."

"I'm not alone," Aunt Hildy protested, the pink in
her cheeks deepening as her emotions rose. "I've got
Kizzie and Remy. And besides, Dr. Destrehan said my
ankle will be healed in a few weeks."

An image of her aunt, hurt and alone, lying in the upstairs hall, flashed through Jill's mind. Had it not been for Remy seeing the flickering lights by mere chance, who knew how long Hildy could have been stranded? What if she had been more badly hurt? What if she had died that night? Jill knew if that had happened she never would have forgiven herself. She was also bound and determined that it not happen again, no matter how long or how hard she had to fight to ensure her aunt's safety and well-being.

Privately, Jill was hoping Hildy would like having a companion so much that she would agree to make the situation a permanent one. Then she would never have to worry about her aunt remaining unattended again. And if Hildy would agree to live in New York with Jill, too, life would be perfect. "Kizzie's not all that reliable," Jill said quietly.

"So she's a little eccentric," Hildy scoffed.

"Aren't we all," Remy drawled. He folded his arms in front of him, taking Hildy's side.

Jill whirled on him, her fury mounting. Damn him for making her life harder than it already was. Couldn't he see she was trying to do what was best for her aunt? "You stay out of this, you big Cajun thug!"

"Jill, for heaven's sake!" Hildy pressed a hand to her chest as if she were about to get an attack of the vapors at any second. "Where are your manners?"

Hildy's chastising voice brought Jill swiftly back to earth. She hadn't been brought up that way, she knew. True Southern ladies were genteel to a fault. True Southern ladies served tea out of silver services, belonged to garden clubs and could make a meal fit for a king in under an hour, under both the best and the worst of circumstances. True Southern ladies did not rant and rave or let roguish men get to them. True Southern ladies kept their composure at all times.

Jill swallowed again. "I'm sorry, Aunt Hildy," she said in a much more subdued tone. Ignoring Remy's equally disgruntled look—what did she care if he was unhappy with her?—Jill tried one more time to talk some sense into her beloved great-aunt. "But we have to talk about this, just as I had to talk to Dr. Destrehan. Aunt Hildy, I know how much you value your independence, and believe me, I would never try to take that away from you. Nor would I ever ask you to give up your home here in Louisiana."

"You wouldn't?"

"No," Jill reassured her aunt softly. She tightened her hands over Hildy's hand. "I know how much you love Magnolia Place and I think you should continue to maintain the house as a country home and family retreat. I just want you to return with me to New York and possibly even live with me in New York, most of the time. Think of it. I could take you to the studio with me as much as you wanted. Think of all the tapings you could watch, the parties you could attend, the actors you could meet."

"Well, that does sound tempting, Jill." Her anxiety fading, Hildy regarded her affectionately. "And you know how much I've enjoyed visiting the show and meeting the actors and going to your parties whenever I am in New York, but I don't think I could live in a skyscraper all the time, honey. I need to be out in the fresh air. I need my garden. I need my own private space," Aunt Hildy finished emphatically.

Out of the corner of her eye, Jill could see the triumphant expression on Remy's face. Deliberately, she ignored it and concentrated on her aunt. "Well, what if I bought a big house with a garden in Connecticut?" Jill asked, bringing up an idea she'd already given considerable thought. "I could even build you a temperature-controlled greenhouse, so you could garden all-year-round." She really wanted Hildy to be happy.

Hildy frowned. "Wouldn't that mean you'd have to commute into the city to work, though?"

"Yes, but I could take the train. It's really no big deal. What is important is that I know you're okay," Jill said.

Hildy patted Jill's arm. "I know my fall upset you."

"Very much," Jill admitted, as tears of remembered misery gathered in her eyes. Hildy was the only family she had now. She didn't know what she would do without her.

"And you know I love you, don't you?" Hildy persevered. Too choked up to speak, Jill nodded. "But I just can't leave Louisiana," her aunt continued. "I wouldn't be comfortable in Connecticut, and with you at the studio all day…honey, it just wouldn't work. I have my friends here, and my garden club." Hildy paused. "We'll work something out, so you won't have to worry. I promise."

Jill didn't want anyone else taking care of Hildy. But maybe that was selfish of her, too. She fell silent, her thoughts and feelings in a jumble. Maybe she had been wrong to go at this full tilt, she thought wearily, ignoring Remy's smug look. Maybe she should just take it one step at a time, Jill thought. Maybe in time her aunt would warm to the idea of moving north. In the meantime, Jill would most likely have to return to New York shortly after Hildy was home from the hospital again. So, like it or not, some temporary arrangements would have to be made. Maybe she should just concentrate on that.

Jill swallowed around the tight knot of suppressed emotion gathering in her throat. "How about getting some live-in help, then, at least for the time being, until your arm comes out of that cast?" she suggested gently, thinking of the list of names Carole Destrehan had given her.

Without warning, Hildy's expression became contrary. She released her hold on Jill's arm. "I don't want anyone underfoot all the time," she said stubbornly, reasserting her independent nature. "And besides, we have bigger problems to tend to."

Jill couldn't imagine what those would be. "Like what?" Jill asked with a confused frown.

"It's my turn to host the weekly garden club meeting on Saturday," Hildy said.

Jill struggled to contain her impatience. "Aunt Hildy, surely the ladies don't expect you to still have the meeting at Magnolia Place now that you're in the hospital."

"Well, whether they expect it or not, I'm going to do it. That is, with your help." Aunt Hildy turned to Remy. "Remy, sweetheart, you'll help Jill prepare for the party, won't you? And videotape it for me? We've got a botanist coming to tell us all about a new disease-resistant strain of azaleas.''

Remy flashed Hildy a million-watt smile as he moved away from the window, and a little closer to the bed. "I'll be glad to help Jill prepare for the party, Hildy."

"Thank you, darlin'. I knew I could count on you."

Jill stepped forward, positioning herself between Remy and her aunt. She'd had about enough of Remy Beauregard's interference. "Are you sure that's wise, Aunt Hildy? I mean, the rewiring in the house still isn't finished and won't be for several weeks." What did Jill know about the garden club? She had usually tried to make herself scarce during the interminably long meetings about seeds and fertilizers and pruning methods.

"Jill, will you please stop worrying?" Aunt Hildy chided. "I am sure everything will be fine. Not that we'll need lights, since the party is going to be in the midafternoon. And we can even hold it outside, if the weather is nice."

Jill and Remy stayed a while longer. Jill took notes on the luncheon menu her aunt wanted served to the garden club. Remy helped her aunt fill out her menu for the following day and then they chatted about inconsequential things until Frieda Davenport arrived.

Frieda was an old friend of Jill's aunt. She owned several flower shops and, at sixty-three, was just getting ready to retire. "How are you doing, Frieda?" Jill said, exchanging hugs with the slender dark-haired woman.

"Not too bad," Frieda said. "Although I'm wondering what I'm going to be doing with myself a month from now when the sale papers are signed and I no longer have a business to run to every day."

"I thought you were going to start off retirement by taking a cruise around the world," Hildy said.

Frieda waved a hand. "I was. But then I got to thinking about it and decided it'd be no fun to go alone."

"Well, don't look at me," Hildy joked. "They won't even let me out of my wheelchair."

Frieda handed Hildy a beautiful bouquet of yellow roses, and bent to kiss her old friend's cheek. "Speaking of feeling better," Frieda said, "maybe we should wait to have the garden club meeting that was scheduled for your place."

"Not on your life," Hildy said firmly. "Jill and Remy have already agreed to help, so it will go on as scheduled, and I plan to be there, too, even if it means bringing a nurse along with me."

"That's the spirit," Frieda said, grinning. "With that kind of attitude, Hildy, you'll be fully recovered in no time."

Because it was obvious that Frieda and Hildy had a lot to talk about, Jill told her aunt she would be back in the morning to see her, and she got ready to leave.

"Remy, sweetheart, see Jill safely to her car, would you?" Hildy said.

It was all Jill could do not to cringe at her aunt's obvious matchmaking. Remy seemed to feel no resentment as he pushed lazily to his feet. "Sure thing, Hildy." He flashed Jill a million-watt smile.

Jill frowned and exited the room.

Remy said a charming goodbye to the ladies, then joined her at the elevator.

As soon as they were alone, Jill spoke her mind. "You may think you've persuaded me otherwise," she said as the elevator doors slid shut, "but you haven't. I'm not giving up on the idea of moving my aunt north to be with me." Jill folded her arms in front of her contentiously and stared straight ahead. "It's just going to take a little longer than I thought for Aunt Hildy to get used to the idea, that's all."

Remy leaned against the opposite wall, his eyes on hers. "You know, Jill," he said in a soft soothing voice that had her turning reluctantly to face him, "Hildy and I may not be related by blood, but she's my neighbor and I love her just as much as you do. Enough to want to see her be able to stay in her native environment for the rest of her life, however long that'll be. I'm not doing this to thwart you, as you seem to think. I'm doing this because she wouldn't be happy away from all her friends."

His words struck a nerve. Worse, it infuriated Jill that her aunt could be so thoroughly dependent on a man who had just moved in next door six months or so ago, a man Jill hadn't even met until the previous day. "She would be so happy if she gave it even half a chance," Jill argued back as the elevator ground to a halt and the doors slid open. Jill stalked out into the lobby, Remy hot on her heels. "They have garden clubs in Connecticut. Aunt Hildy could join them and make new friends. And she could visit her old friends whenever we came back to Magnolia Place. Or they could come north and stay with us and visit her there. Furthermore, Remy, Aunt Hildy has absolutely loved staying with me every time she's visited!''

"There's a hell of a lot of difference between visiting somewhere and actually living there,'' Remy retorted as he breezed through the doors after her, out into the dark night. Falling into step next to her, he adjusted his strides to her shorter ones.

Jill stalked down the sidewalk, then stomped across the drive to the parking lot. "She could at least give it a try."

Remy caught Jill by the elbow and spun her around to face him. "You could at least try to see things from her point of view and accept that she would never, in her entire life, be happy cooped up in a strange house in a strange city while you were at work all day."

The empathy in his dark brown eyes struck a chord in Jill—a guilty one. She knew she had a tendency to run roughshod over others in her desire to get things done. And right now she wanted to get her aunt situated safely. Trying not to think how warm and strong and sure his hands felt on her arms, she tilted her head up to his, and then stepped back, out of reach.

"Okay, maybe I did jump the gun, pushing Aunt Hildy to think about the idea of my buying a place for both of us in Connecticut," she said regretfully. "Maybe we shouldn't talk about her moving north permanently for at least another year or two. Maybe we should just concentrate on getting her a reliable companion to get her through the next several months, and then when she's adjusted to the idea of having live-in help, go from there."

Remy looped his thumbs through the belt loops on his jeans and regarded her with unchecked disapproval. "You've got everything figured out, haven't you?" he said, very low.

Jill's jaw thrust out stubbornly. There was nothing she hated more than being judged. "I'm trying," she said.

Remy sighed, his frustration with her, and the situation, evident. "Too bad you're not letting your aunt in on any of the decisions that will so radically affect her life," he said.

Jill tossed her head and sent him a withering glance. "I'm just trying to do what's best!" she stormed.

Remy quirked a dissenting brow, as her silky brown hair settled around her upturned face. "Best for Hildy, Jill?" he said quietly. "Or best for you?"

REMY'S WORDS RANG in Jill's ears the entire drive home.

He is not going to make me feel guilty about this. I am trying to do what is best for my aunt. I am not being selfish here. I am not trying to make her miserable. I am just trying to ensure that the quality of the last years of her life is every bit as good as the rest of her life was. I have nothing to be ashamed about, no matter what that low-down, sneaky, ingratiating skunk Remy Beauregard would imply.

So caught up was Jill in her mental argument, that it wasn't until she was almost home that she noticed he was right behind her. Again. She passed his place, a ranch house she'd seen only from the road. As she had feared, he didn't turn into his own driveway. The thought of having him underfoot again made Jill's temper soar even more. She drove on to Magnolia Place, parked in front of the house and slammed out of her car. Behind her, Remy got out of his pickup.

"It wasn't necessary for you to follow me home," Jill said stiffly as she strode up the front walk.

Remy fell into step beside her. To Jill's amazement he seemed to have forgotten they had ever quarreled. "Since it's after dark, Hildy would expect me to do the gentlemanly thing and see you to the door," he reported laconically, taking her elbow as she moved up the steps that led to the front door. "Besides, I wanted to make sure you got in safely."

Jill used her new key to unlock the door, then put a hand out to bar his way into the house. "You're not coming in, Remy. Not tonight," she said. And she meant it.

Kizzie stepped from the shadows. "But he must come in," Kizzie said. "I've prepared a dinner for the both of you, just like Miz Hildy told me I should."

Jill thought of the three versions of Felicity and Beau's breakup scene that she had to review, not to mention the soap bible she still had to finish, and knew that, like it or not, she was going to have to eat to get any work done. Besides, this was Kizzie's first halfway friendly overture since she had arrived. Jill could hardly risk offending her by rejecting it. "When did you talk to my aunt?" Jill asked.

"Half an hour ago. She told me to make sure and feed you both before I leave."

"That's Hildy," Remy said with an appreciative grin. "Always thinking of someone else." He pried

Jill's fingers from the doorframe, lifted her arm and sauntered on into the house. A fuming Jill was left to follow.

Her steps unusually fast and purposeful, Kizzie headed for the dining room. "I put the food in here," she said.

Jill remained where she was. She didn't know what it was exactly, but something here seemed really amiss. Remy seemed to read her mind. He bent and whispered in her ear, "I'd think twice before I offended her again, sugar. Kizzie's as powerful an enemy as she is a friend. Besides," Remy continued with a friendly wink, his warm breath brushing her ear, "what can one meal hurt?"

Jill had already been pushed around as much as she could endure by the appealing Cajun. "Plenty," she snapped, "when the meal's taken with a miserable low-down ingratiating skunk like you."

Remy's laughter rumbled in her ear. He ducked his head in mock sheepishness. "Aw, you're just saying that to make me feel good, sugar," he teased.

Jill glared at him, her heart pounding. There was no way this man was ever going to kiss her again, she promised herself firmly. "Don't you just wish," she snapped.

The table was set with Aunt Hildy's best linen, silver and china. Candles glowed softly. Kizzie waited next to the table, her hands folded in front of her.

Jill thought of Aunt Hildy and moved to the table. Remy was right. Jill couldn't afford to hurt Kizzie's feelings again. And it was only one meal. Clearly, the eccentric housekeeper had gone to a lot of trouble here ... maybe because Hildy had heard how awfully the two were getting along and had talked some sense into Kizzie. The least Jill could do was be appreciative.

"This is lovely, Kizzie," she said. "Thank you."

Remy held out a chair for Jill. She slid into it self-consciously while Kizzie tossed the salad and took the lid off a silver chafing dish filled with a savory mixture of shrimp, sausage, crabs, chicken, spices, vegetables and rice. Jambalaya, Jill's favorite Cajun dish. When she finished serving them, Kizzie retreated to the far corner of the room, crossed her arms in front of her and stood stoically by.

Remy and Jill ate in silence. When they were done with the delicious meal, and had nearly polished off the chocolate torte she had prepared for dessert, Kizzie brought out a carafe of what looked to be an after-dinner liqueur and two glasses. Jill watched as Kizzie filled the two glasses and returned to the far corner of the room.

Remy grinned at Jill. "The dinner was fantastic, Kizzie," he said over his shoulder. He then picked up his wineglass. "And to you, my darling Jill. *Laissez les bon temps rouler,*" he said, touching the rim of his wineglass to hers. "Let the good times roll."

Jill wasn't about to toast to good times with Remy, so she made her own toast. "To Aunt Hildy's speedy recovery."

"Amen to that," Remy agreed.

Their eyes locked, they each lifted their glasses to their lips. Feeling ridiculously relieved that this dinner with Remy was over, Jill sipped, then choked as the fiery, foul-tasting liqueur filled her mouth and slid down her throat to her stomach. Her eyes stinging, she stared at Remy and fought to catch her breath.

Kizzie smiled triumphantly. She took off the apron that covered her faded cotton housedress. "*Now* you have a reason to stay," Kizzie told Jill mysteriously. Kizzie looked at Remy. "And you have a reason to keep an eye on *la jolie fille,*" she said. Her expression smug, Kizzie slipped from the room.

"What'd she call me?" Jill asked Remy.

"The pretty girl," Remy replied absently as he stared at his glass and shook his head.

"What's going on here, Remy?" Jill asked suspiciously. "What did Kizzie mean when she said I now have a reason to stay?" Jill didn't know why—maybe it was the amused yet wary expression on Remy's face—but she was beginning to feel the first stirrings of panic. Yet Remy wasn't acting as if they'd just been poisoned. Quite the opposite.

"Kizzie was referring to the drink." Remy studied the glass, then took another sip. Unlike Jill, he did not make a face at the spicy taste of the garlic-flavored liqueur, even when he drained the entire glass and set it down on the table.

"What is this?" Jill asked, holding up her half-filled glass. Now that she took a good look at it, it looked green and smelled ever so slightly like Pernod. But if it *was* Pernod, Jill thought, it had been tampered with—a lot.

Remy watched her carefully. His eyes were suddenly sparkling with a mischief that Jill found even more unnerving than the vile taste of the liqueur she'd just downed so naively. "Sure you want to know, sugar?" Remy teased. "This might be one case where ignorance truly is bliss."

"I'm positive I want to know," Jill said firmly.

Remy's grin widened unrepentantly. "Unless I'm mistaken, it's Kizzie's very famous, ultrapotent, Love Potion #5."

Chapter Four

"Argh!" Jill screamed and dashed to the kitchen. She swallowed a mouthful of water, swished it around in her mouth, then spit it out in the sink.

Remy lounged beside her, his mouth crooked up in amusement. He wasn't the least bit concerned about the noxious concoction they'd both just imbibed. "Won't do any good, sugar," he drawled. "You already drank the potion."

I still have to try, Jill thought. She took another gulp of cold water, swished it around and spit it into the sink. "What's in it?" she said between ragged breaths. "Or do I really want to know?"

Remy looked perfectly at ease, in fact pleased, with the turn of events. "I'm guessing, as the actual ingredients are top secret, but probably garlic to lure a lover, ginseng for sexual stimulation, coriander for sexual power and Pernod for its intoxicating benefits. Don't look so panicked. It's just simple Cajun folk magic. There's nothing in that potion that will hurt us."

"Speak for yourself," Jill muttered beneath her breath. She was already plenty upset.

"Why, Jill, I never would have figured you for the superstitious type," Remy drawled.

Jill stalked to the drawer that contained the clean kitchen linens and pulled out a white linen napkin. "What's that supposed to mean?"

"If you believe in the potion as much as your ashen color says you do...then it means we're doomed now, sugar."

"Very funny." Jill blotted the dampness from her lips. "But you're right about one thing." She straightened slowly, then frowned as she realized her knees felt a little wobbly. "We are in trouble if that potion works, cause we're a match made in hell, Remy."

"I don't know about that." Remy surprised her by taking her into his arms. "No doubt about it, you're a handful," he murmured as his glance skimmed her upturned face. "But as for the rest—" He looked down at her longingly. "As for the rest, I think I could handle it," he said softly.

But I couldn't, Jill thought, as the warmth of him radiated outward, enveloping her everywhere they touched, inch by seductive inch. *You've barely touched me, Remy, and already my heart is pounding uncontrollably.* She splayed her hands across his chest, and fought to regain control of her senses. "Remy—" Her low voice carried a warning as she stepped back and came up short, against the sink.

He sighed and released her reluctantly. "You're right. It wouldn't be fair to put the moves on you when you're under the spell."

Jill slowly got her bearings. She was stunned to realize how disappointed she was that Remy hadn't kissed her. Surely, she couldn't be hoping for a tryst with her aunt's reptilian neighbor, Jill thought as she pushed a shaky hand through her hair, restoring the soft dark cloud to some semblance of order. Was it possible there was some magic in Kizzie's love potion after all? she wondered nervously.

Furious for allowing herself to fall victim, even for a millisecond, to Kizzie's superstitious antics, Jill scowled at Remy. Her temper flared white-hot. "Out!" She pointed to the door.

Remy grinned and pushed his fingers through the windswept layers of his sandy brown hair. "I can see you need time to digest all that's happened tonight," he allowed with mock solemnity. He started for the door, his strides long and lazy. "I'll come back tomorrow, when you've had time to calm down and accept the inevitable," he promised.

"There's nothing to accept!" Jill fumed. But it was too late; he'd already left.

JILL HAD BEEN at her computer for almost eight hours when Kizzie showed up the next afternoon. "Hold it right there, Kizzie." Jill stopped typing and stood. She regarded Kizzie determinedly. "I want to talk to you."

Kizzie just looked at her. "I got vegetables to clean." She stomped toward the kitchen, her black combat boots making heavy thudding noises on the parquet floor.

Throwing a glance skyward, praying for the patience to deal with her aunt's wayward housekeeper,

Jill followed. "Kizzie, I want you to take that spell off Remy and me this instant!" she ordered firmly.

"What spell?" Kizzie feigned innocence as she tied on an apron over her faded housedress.

"That love potion you made for me last night," Jill specified tightly.

"I thought you didn't believe in Cajun folk magic," Kizzie said slyly.

Jill worked feverishly to keep a sweat from breaking out on her brow. She wished she weren't just the tiniest bit superstitious, but deep down, she knew she was. She never walked under a ladder if she could help it, she crossed the street if she saw a black cat and she absolutely refused to open an umbrella indoors. "I don't believe in folk magic, Cajun or otherwise," Jill told Kizzie, and then told herself it was mostly true. "But Remy does, and he'll never leave me alone unless you take that spell off of us!"

Kizzie removed an armful of leafy green vegetables from the crisper drawer in the refrigerator and carried them serenely to the sink. "I can't do that."

Jill watched in mounting frustration as Kizzie began to rinse celery. "Why not?"

Kizzie turned partway to face Jill and waved a leafy green stick in her face. "Because Miz Hildy told me to do it."

"What?" Jill was aghast.

"She said you need love in your life. And I think so, too."

"That is utterly ridiculous," Jill fumed, moving nearer.

"I don't think so. I don't want Miz Hildy to leave Louisiana," Kizzie said, as she finished the celery and began scrubbing the zucchini. "If you stay here to be with Remy, then Miz Hildy will stay here, too. And that will make us all happy."

Jill realized abruptly that she wasn't the only person who loved her aunt. Suddenly, that made it a lot easier to deal with Kizzie's obstinate behavior. "Oh, Kizzie, it's not like she'll be going away forever," Jill said gently. "Aunt Hildy and I will come back several times a year to visit. You can even keep your job here, if that's what you're worried about."

Kizzie frowned and scrubbed the zucchini with more than necessary force. "I don't care about the house, I care about Miz Hildy, and I don't want you taking her away!" Kizzie set the zucchini on the chopping board.

Jill sensed a major battle brewing. It was going to be hard enough convincing her aunt to return to New York with her, even for a few months, without Kizzie and Remy both in the middle, trying to keep it from happening.

"Hey, y'all." Remy appeared in the door, his tool belt clanking around his waist. "Thought I heard voices in here." He bent to kiss Kizzie's weathered cheek. "Got any more of that delicious potion for me to drink?" he teased.

"As a matter of fact..." Kizzie started for the refrigerator. Jill watched, still fuming, as the housekeeper pulled a dark green bottle from the very back of the refrigerator. Kizzie eyed Jill speculatively. "Looks like Miz Jill could use some more potion, too," she said.

"Forget it," Jill said firmly.

Remy grinned. He folded his arms in front of him in a way that only made more of the muscled contours of his chest, then grinned at Jill. "I'll take some."

The last thing they needed was Remy drinking a Pernod-laced Cajun aphrodisiac; he was wild and mischievous enough as it was. "Like hell you will." Jill grabbed Remy's arm before Kizzie could so much as get out a glass or hand the elixir over to him. Her hand curving determinedly over the solidness of his bicep, she dragged him out of the kitchen. "Kizzie, I will talk to you later," Jill said over her shoulder. Kizzie muttered back talk in Cajun French while Jill dragged Remy out onto the front porch. As soon as she had him where she wanted him, she dropped her hands and planted both hands on her hips. "Honestly, Remy, don't you think we have enough problems without you encouraging Kizzie to play around with that Cajun folk magic?"

Remy pushed his cap back on his head. Today's model was black and bronze and was emblazoned with the New Orleans Saints logo. "You know what they say. One man's problems are another's heaven."

Jill flushed despite herself. "I mean it," she said, edging back slightly from the woodsy male scent of him. "You've got to stop egging her on about this."

Remy quirked a dissenting sandy brow. "Egging her on or egging you on?"

Jill blew out an impatient breath. She was not going to let Remy, or that sexy bad-boy grin of his, get to her. "I want to know what we're going to do about this," she persisted.

He cocked his head to the side, as if he were the one whose patience was being tried. "Why should we do anything?"

"Because!" Jill said, flushing despite herself. She was irritated he was making her spell it out for him. "If we don't do something to negate Kizzie's Cajun folk magic, then she's going to keep up the running verbal commentary. You may not care about it, but I have to live here, and listen to it while I'm trying to work. So I would appreciate it if we could put an end to the banter about Kizzie's Love Potion #5 once and for all."

"I see your point." Remy rubbed his jaw contemplatively. "And I suppose, if you're so all-fired determined to get out of this..." His reluctance to end the shenanigans was evident.

"I am!"

He shrugged his broad shoulders laconically. "I guess I could offer up a solution, of sorts."

"I'm listening."

He grasped her arm above the elbow and tugged her close. "Kizzie's not about to give us the antidote to her love potion, but that doesn't mean we can't get one," he murmured in a low, syrupy voice as he cast a surreptitious look at the windows behind him.

Jill knew they didn't need an antidote; Kizzie's potion was harmless. But as far as Kizzie was concerned, they did. Her hopes rose as she finally saw a way out of their predicament. She stood on tiptoe and whispered into his ear, "You know somebody?"

Remy nodded solemnly.

"Who?"

"Gator Dupres. He lives over in the Atchafalaya Swamp."

Gator, Jill thought. Another swamp person. Someone whose folk magic Kizzie would respect. Perfect. "Okay, let's go," she said, already heading back inside to turn off her computer.

Remy caught her arm and reeled her back in to his side. He shook his head, vetoing the idea. "Gator'll need at least a day to cook up an antidote."

Jill was disappointed. She'd been looking forward to getting the folk magic spell off them immediately, even if that meant she had to spend the entire evening with Remy. "But I suppose we could go tomorrow evening," Remy continued, "say about five or so."

Jill tried not to notice how warm her skin was getting where he still had a hold on her arm. She tried not to feel the warmth of him, or see the sensuality in the soft firm lines of his mouth. "And in the meantime?"

Remy shrugged and belatedly dropped his hand. "In the meantime, sugar, we suffer."

His response wasn't what she had hoped for, but she, too, knew no other way to bring Kizzie back into line. Jill sighed. She supposed that would have to do. "I suppose you're here to do more work on the rewiring?"

Remy nodded. "I'd like to get your aunt's bedroom finished, and maybe start on the hall bath next."

That settled it for Jill. If Remy was going to be underfoot, roaming from room to room, his tool belt jangling as he moved, she wouldn't be able to concentrate a lick. "Don't worry about me being in your way. As soon as I turn off my computer, I'm going over to the hospital to see my aunt. I'll probably spend the entire evening with Hildy and come home very late."

Or in other words, she was trying to tell him as subtly as she could not to wait around for the chance to tease her mercilessly. She was through playing games with Remy Beauregard.

Remy's eyes darkened again, but Jill couldn't quite read his expression. Finally he shrugged, as if it didn't matter to him either way. "Give Hildy my best" was all he said.

"Is REMY STILL WORKING on the rewiring?" Hildy asked, as soon as Jill entered the hospital room.

Jill set down the basket of fresh fruit she'd brought with her, and handed over a new armload of magazines for her aunt. "Yes, he is."

"So how's the rewiring coming?" Hildy continued with a mischievous grin.

"Fine. Although given the amount of work involved in doing each room, it's going to take days for him to finish." Unfortunately, Jill couldn't complain about the drawn-out nature of the repairs, because Remy was doing the work for free after he had finished his paying jobs each and every day.

"While we're on the subject of Remy Beauregard, I have a bone to pick with you."

"Oh?" Hildy gave Jill a look of complete innocence.

Jill propped both her hands on her hips. "Kizzie told me that you instructed her to make a love potion and give it to Remy and me last night as an after-dinner cordial."

"Oh, yes...that." Hildy waved her acknowledgment.

"'Oh, yes...that'?" Jill repeated.

"Kizzie and I were just trying to be helpful," Hildy explained.

Jill blew out an exasperated breath. "Helpful, how?"

"Well, dear, you don't have a lot of time here, and frankly, your budding romance with Remy needed a little boost. Kizzie's Love Potion #5 is legendary for its effectiveness, so..." Hildy smiled. "We gave it to you."

Jill adjusted the blinds so a little less light was coming in. "I never would have taken even a sip of the vile elixir had I just known what it was," Jill declared, turning back to her aunt.

Hildy lifted a snowy white brow, as if to dispute that statement. Then she smiled in a knowing, maternal way. "Remy says it's already working."

Jill rolled her eyes and tried desperately to keep the heat of embarrassment out of her cheeks. Somehow, through sheer strength of will, she managed. "Remy exaggerates," Jill replied coolly.

"I don't know. There's a bit of life in your eyes to-day."

Jill knew she was agitated. She'd been agitated ever since she'd imbibed the potion. She'd been agitated since that first kiss in her bedroom. She still couldn't believe he'd done that, or worse, that she had responded as she had. It wasn't like her to be so reckless—not at all.

Jill smiled at her aunt, determined to let her know she was taking charge of the situation. "Not to worry, Aunt Hildy. Remy and I are going to get an antidote tomorrow evening."

Aunt Hildy made a disbelieving sound. "I didn't know there was an antidote for love," Hildy said.

"Remy and I are not in love!" Jill exclaimed hotly as she adjusted her aunt's pillows and straightened the blankets on her bed.

Her aunt merely smiled. "Really?" Hildy murmured, as if greatly perplexed. "You could have fooled me."

"I AM NOT GOING TO LET these silly superstitions get to me," Jill told herself firmly as she returned home close to midnight. The hospital had allowed her to stay long past visiting hours, and she'd ended up dozing off in a chair beside Hildy's bed. Waking stiff and sore, she had kissed her sleeping aunt goodbye and headed out to her car. The twenty-five-minute drive home had cleared her head and the nap had given her a much-needed rest. Unfortunately, as a consequence of both, she was no longer sleepy at all.

Experience told Jill she'd had just enough sleep to make going to sleep again anytime soon impossible. Deciding to make good use of her newfound energy—even if it was nervous energy—Jill headed for the kitchen and put on a pot of tea. She figured she could get in another couple hours of work, and then go to bed.

Remy and Kizzie had both gone home for the day, so the house was blissfully quiet as she headed for her computer. No sooner had the computer booted up, however, than it and the lights went dead. Jill swore as pitch-blackness descended, and then swore again as she stumbled around in the dark, looking for the phone. "Darn that Remy," she muttered as she punched in his number. "I bet he did this to me on purpose!"

He answered on the second ring, sounding as if he, too, were wide-awake. "Hello."

"Remy, you scoundrel. You conniving, sneaky, underhanded rake—"

"Sugar, I love the compliments," he interrupted with a deeply amused chuckle, "but you sound upset."

"That's because I *am* upset!" Jill fumed, as her eyes slowly adjusted to the pitch-black darkness of the house. "What did you do to the lights?"

"What do you mean, what did I do to the lights?" he asked.

Jill ignored the puzzled undertone in his sexy voice. Everything about the man, the way he moved and smiled and kissed, said he was a master at seducing women...a master at making women think they needed him. Only she knew better. She didn't need Remy in her life, any more than she had needed her sly, conniving father. "I switched on my computer and I am now sitting alone in the dark."

There was a pause. "Are you trying to tell me your lights went out?" Remy probed.

"Every one of them," Jill confirmed. Realizing she was gritting her teeth, she forced herself to relax her jaw. "So what'd you do to them?" Phone in hand, she paced back and forth restlessly, her heels making clicking noises on the parquet floor.

"Sugar, I didn't do anything that would cause that to happen. But don't worry," he promised in a low, soothing tone before Jill could get a word in edgewise. "I'll be right over." The phone clicked.

Jill stood at the window, gripping the phone. Now that her eyes had adjusted, there was just enough moonlight filtering in through the windows to allow her to walk back to her desk and put the receiver back in its cradle. She should have figured that Remy, ever the opportunist, would rig things so he could come charging to her rescue. But he had another think coming if he figured she was going to go all needy and helpless in his arms. She would get him to fix the lights; then she would promptly offer her thanks and show him the door.

As REMY DROVE UP, he could see the flickering candlelight in the downstairs windows of Magnolia Place. That was reassuring, but he knew he wouldn't be able to relax completely until he had made absolutely certain that Jill was all right. Although she had been doing her best to sound fiesty and in control of the situation on the phone, she had sounded on edge.

He cut the motor on the truck and slammed out of it. The front door opened wide as he took the steps up to the porch two and three at a time.

Jill stood before him, her hands on her hips. She was still dressed in the powder blue business suit she'd been wearing earlier in the day, and she had Hildy's heavy-duty flashlight in her hand. "I hope you can fix this quickly," she said.

Remy read the accusation in her dark blue eyes. Irritated, he strode past Jill and into the front hall. He reached for the row of switches beside the door, and one by one, hit every one of them. Nothing happened.

"I told you the lights aren't working," Jill complained with a scowl. She tossed her head. Her mahogany hair flew around her like a fluffy cap before settling back into place. Remy enjoyed the view a second more before he spoke.

"I like to experience things for myself." *Including you, Miss Jill Sutherland,* he thought, as he checked her out from head to toe. Her cheeks were flushed, her lips were bare and she was furious about the loss of power at Magnolia Place. Furious because she suspected he might be behind it. "Did you check the fuse box?" he asked.

"Not yet." Jill strode past, the accordion pleats on her short skirt twirling out as she moved.

Remy tore his glance from the curvaceous muscles flexing in her slender legs, and forced his mind back to business. "Why not?"

Jill scowled. "I can't recall where it is," she mumbled, barely loud enough for him to hear. "I thought it was down in the basement, but . . . I guess not."

So much for self-sufficiency, Remy thought. Jill needed him tonight whether she liked it or not.

Seizing the opportunity to tease her, he said, "Sure about that?" He turned and started laconically back down the steps.

"What do you mean?" She switched on her flashlight and followed him around the side of the house, moving agilely through the soft, damp ankle-high grass.

"I mean, are you sure you weren't just afraid to come out here all by your lonesome and check the switches?" Remy teased.

Jill glowered at him. "Very funny." Clamping her arms in front of her, she drew the thigh-skimming suit jacket closer to her breasts. "Can't you hurry this up?" she demanded bad-temperedly.

Grinning triumphantly because he knew he'd gotten to her—again—Remy opened the metal cover to the fuse box. "Well, here's your problem," he drawled in a voice thicker than molasses.

"What?" Curious, Jill moved in a tad closer and stood on tiptoe to see.

Remy moved slightly to the side. With a hand on Jill's shoulder, he guided her closer to the box so he could show her what he'd found, so she would know how to fix it herself next time. "Someone has turned off all your switches. All you have to do is this." He hit them, one by one, and the lights in the house came on. He shut the cover to the fuse box.

Jill immediately became irate again. "You, you—"

Remy knew how her mind worked. Jill would like nothing better than to blame him for all the feelings rolling around inside her. And while he admitted he had done his best to stir things up, he hadn't done this. "Hey," he said, thumping his chest emphatically, "I had nothing to do with this. As you very well know, I was home, minding my own business, when your lights went out."

"Then who hit my fuses?" she demanded. Remy shrugged. "Kizzie!" Jill said. "My aunt might even have told her to do it, as a way of further pushing the two of us together."

Remy's eyes lit with interest. "You think so?"

Jill scowled. "Heaven knows my aunt hasn't missed an opportunity to matchmake for the two of us yet, even from her hospital bed!" she muttered.

Remy couldn't deny that Hildy and Kizzie might do something like that, if the two of them thought there was something, such as a romance between Remy and Jill, to be gained. He also saw a chance to have a little fun with this as Kizzie and Hildy, bless their ornery hearts, probably suspected he might when presented with the opportunity.

"Good try at shifting the blame, Jill," Remy drawled as he wheeled on Jill. Playing the aggrieved victim to the hilt, he poked his finger at her chest. "But how do I know *you* didn't set *me* up?"

"What?" Jill sputtered, stunned.

"You heard me!" His look every bit as accusing as hers had been upon his arrival at Magnolia Place, he backed her all the way to the side of the house. When her back brushed the wall, he put his arms up on either side of her and leaned in close so their faces were but inches apart. "How do I know you didn't mess with your own fuse box?" he interrogated playfully, thinking how pretty she looked with the moonlight silvering her face and her hair.

"Why would I do that?" Jill demanded as she angled her head back.

Enjoying the soft rose fragrance that was Jill, Remy shrugged. "I don't know." He leaned even closer and speculated suspiciously, "Maybe you wanted to get me over here and any excuse would do. Your aunt Hildy has sure been pushing me your way."

Jill couldn't deny that. "I had nothing to do with Hildy's matchmaking!" Jill fumed. "As for the other..." Jill laughed indignantly. "You have the wildest imagination!"

"Do I?" Remy leaned in another half inch closer. "Am I imagining this?" He traced the delicate profile of her face with the back of his hand and watched her tremble. A thrill went through him as he realized how responsive she was to his touch. "Am I imagining the effect the love potion has had on you, or the fact that ever since you drank it last night you've been as nervous as a long-tailed cat in a room full of rocking chairs whenever you're around me?"

Jill looked down her nose at him, her adrenaline flowing. Losing her temper, she retorted hotly, "Kizzie's love potion didn't do a damn thing. I was already feeling that way before—" Her expression panicked, she tried to slide beneath his outstretched arm.

He lowered it as she moved, and delighting in her closeness, caught her before she could flee. "So now we know," he said slowly, deliberately teasing her even more, just to watch her blush. "All along it's been you, Jill, behind your aunt's matchmaking, then the potion, and now the lights!" He regarded her boldly. "All along you've been after me! And you even enlisted your aunt and Kizzie's help!"

"Dream on!" Jill put a closed fist on his sternum and pushed with all her might.

Remy got her message, but he enjoyed holding her too much to budge, at least right away. "You swear to me you're not part of this matchmaking scheme?" he questioned solemnly.

Jill blew out an exasperated breath and tossed her head again. "Of course I'm not!"

"Then who—?"

"It must be Kizzie or my aunt, or maybe even both, arranging for the lights to go out so I'd have to call you! But they are wasting their time, because it is not going to work!"

"It already has," Remy disagreed. She shot him a sharp look. He lifted both hands in silent proof. "I'm here, aren't I?" And damn glad he was to be here, too. It meant something, knowing that he was the first person she had called. So he was an electrician. So he lived next door. She still could have called someone else, but she hadn't....

"Well, now that my lights are all back on, you can go home, Remy Beauregard."

Going home was the last thing Remy wanted to do, when Jill was looking so pretty, and acting so fired up.

"I don't know, Jill," he drawled. He wrapped one arm around her waist and pulled her to him, and put his other hand to his brow. "I think I'm finally beginning to feel the effects of Kizzie's potion."

"You are ridiculous, Remy Beauregard," Jill said. But she also tilted her head back to give him a thorough visual assessment.

Remy grinned. Jill might not want to admit it, but she was beginning to care for him, at least on some cursory level. And while that wasn't the kind of concern and attention he wanted from her in the long run, it was a start.

He threaded his hand through the soft cloud of bobbed hair at the nape of her neck. "I'm also under your spell, just like you're under mine, sugar. Admit it, Jill. Whether we meant to take that love potion or not, we are both feeling the effects of Kizzie's Cajun folk magic. Soon, the forces demanding we get together are going to be so strong, we won't be able to fight it."

Jill turned in his arms so that she was facing away from him. She studied the lights that were now blazing inside the house. "Speak for yourself."

Remy placed both hands on her shoulders and gently traced the slenderness of her shape. "You're saying you're completely unaffected?" Remy prodded, daring her to be completely honest with him.

She held her breath a long moment. "Yes."

Liar, Remy thought, as he felt her tremble once more. He spun her around to face him again and held her there when she would have bolted. "Then prove it," he dared, very low.

At the challenging note in his tone, her dark blue eyes gleamed. "If I do, will you stop talking about the potion?"

Remy smiled. "If you can kiss me in a way that neither of us feel anything, then sure, I'll forget about the potion. I'll even forget about the antidote," Remy conceded.

She stared at him in thoughtful silence. Finally she lifted one slender shoulder in an insouciant shrug. "If it gets me out of a trip into the swamp, then *I suppose* I could suffer one more kiss from you. But I warn you," Jill said, with an arch look, "we get to administer this little test my way, on my turf, Remy Beauregard, or not at all."

Remy nodded. He knew Jill wasn't going to stay in Louisiana long. Hell, she wasn't even his type. But he'd take her kisses any way he could get them, for however long he could get them. "Inside or outside the house?" was his only question.

"Inside," Jill said. "It's too cold and damp out here."

Remy knew exactly what she meant. The weather outside was just right for cuddling and kissing, and that was not good, since Jill was determined to do everything and anything possible to spoil the mood.

Chapter Five

Just how did one go about kissing badly? Jill wondered as she led the way back into the house. It wasn't as though she'd never had a bad kiss. She'd had plenty of them. But it had less to do with technique than chemistry and the lack of it, and chemistry was one thing she and Remy weren't in short supply of.

"So, where do you want to do this?" Remy asked, acting as if it were no big deal to him, either.

Jill stopped beneath the chandelier at the entranceway. Her entire insides were knotted with what she sincerely hoped was nerves and *not* anticipation. "Right here is fine."

Remy stood where directed, letting her know with a mischievous glance that he was completely malleable to whatever she suggested. "Hands up or down?"

He was determined to get to her. She was just as determined not to let him. Jill tore her gaze from the sparkling lights in his dark brown eyes. "Doesn't matter," she said indifferently.

"Okay, then they'll stay down."

That was a surprise. Jill had expected him to want to take her in his arms. She kept her face carefully expressionless, stood on tiptoe and pressed her closed lips to his. She held them there a cool five seconds, and then, despite the fierce urge to do more, withdrew.

When she lowered her heels to the floor she looked up and offered another cool smile. "See?" she said, her heart pounding, her knees feeling like jelly. "Nothing to it." Except that her lips were still tingling, her whole body was alive and aching and she had never wanted more fiercely to be held, loved, cared for.

"Your way there's nothing to it," he allowed.

"My way is the only way anything's going to happen—or not happen—between us," Jill said firmly. Maybe she was being a bit of a shrew, but she wanted him to know where he stood with her so these games of his would end.

"Hmm." Remy rubbed at the underside of his jaw thoughtfully, never taking his eyes from hers. "I still think we'd better get the antidote."

Considering the fact that she was still tingling from head to toe, Jill was inclined to agree with him. Intellectually, she knew there was nothing to Kizzie's potion except wishful thinking on Kizzie's part. Emotionally, Jill definitely felt that someone had put a spell on her.

"Tomorrow afternoon okay with you?" Remy asked.

Telling herself she wasn't the least bit delighted to have an excuse to spend even more time with Remy, she shrugged. If this would end the attraction between herself and Remy, of course she would go. "If you insist."

"So how far into the swamp is this place?" Jill asked at six the following evening. Now that they were actually here, on the edge of the Atchafalaya Swamp, she was beginning to have second thoughts. The swamp was full of snakes, alligators and all sorts of reptilian wildlife; Jill had never been fond of reptiles...even ones in the zoo.

"It'll take us a good half hour or more to get to Gator's," Remy said. He slipped an unlit Coleman lantern into the front of the pirogue next to the wooden oar, then held out a hand.

Jill stepped into the narrow, canoelike swamp boat and settled herself at one end. She braced her hands on either side of her and inclined her head in the direction of the wooden building on stilts to their left. It looked as if it had been expertly put together from one of those prefab kits, and then allowed to weather naturally to a dark slate gray. "Is that your fishing shack?"

Remy nodded as he pushed the canoe into the water, and then hopped into the front. Dipping the long oar into the water with strong repetitious strokes, he paddled the pirogue toward deeper water.

Jill wasn't surprised at all that he could handle a boat so well; there was a rugged outdoorsmanlike quality about Remy that made his command of the swamp seem perfectly natural. She was a little taken aback, however, that Remy could look so damn sexy wearing just a faded blue oxford cloth shirt and equally worn jeans. But then, it wasn't the clothes eliciting such a reaction from her, she thought, it was the man inside the clothes, all six feet four inches of him. Every cell inside him was solid male muscle and Cajun wildness. And part of her, the impractical highly romantic part of her, was incredibly attracted to that wildness.

So the sooner they got this antidote and swallowed it, the better, she thought determinedly. Maybe the antidote was what it would take to convince Remy of the truth, that his chances of forging any type of relationship with her at all were nil.

"I come out here whenever I want to get back to my roots," Remy said as he guided the pirogue along the murky dark green waters, through an eerie maze of gnarled cypress trees and hyacinths.

Jill settled back as the sun set slowly in the west. "You grew up in a swamp?"

"On the edge of one. These days, my father makes his living running boat tours through the swamps, but when I was growing up he was a crawfisherman. My mom and I used to help him bring in the nets, from the traps."

"You don't have any brothers and sisters?"

"Nope."

"So we're both only children," Jill said.

"Guess so."

"Did you ever wish you had brothers and sisters?"

"All the time. You?"

Jill nodded. "It's lonely, growing up without siblings."

"Yeah, well that's something I've promised myself," Remy allowed with a smile. "When I get married and have kids, I'm having more than one."

Jill was silent. He shot a look at her over his shoulder. "You look surprised," he said as they glided past a foot-wide lotus pad peppered with several brilliant orange Gulf butterflies.

"I guess I *am* surprised," Jill admitted as she listened to the swish of the water against Remy's paddle, and the sounds of wildlife all around them. As they passed an alligator sliding nose first into the water from the opposite bank, she gripped the edges of the boat a little harder. "Part of me can't see you ever getting married."

"That's 'cause you don't know me—yet." Remy looked back at her with a confident smile that said he planned to remedy that. They approached an intersection of several channels. He turned the boat east. "What about you? Are you going to get married again?" Remy asked.

Jill tried not to think about the fact that it was probably going to be dark on the return journey to Remy's fishing shack and his pickup truck. "How do you know I was married even once?"

"Hildy." Remy gave her another intrigued look as they passed beneath a huge live oak tree that dripped with Spanish moss. "She said you were devastated when your marriage ended and that you haven't been serious about anyone since."

Fury coursed through Jill, but she forced herself to present a tranquil front. "Aunt Hildy had no right telling you that."

Remy shrugged as they passed another shack. The inhabitants lifted their hand in a friendly wave. Remy waved back and kept paddling with strong sure strokes. "Hildy was worried because you never seem to date."

Jill looked away from Remy's probing gaze. "I date."

Half of his mouth lifted in a provoking grin. "Business dinners are not dates."

Jill flushed guilty, choosing not to comment on what she couldn't deny. She leaned forward, bringing her blue-jean-covered legs closer to her chest. As darkness fell, there was a definite chill in the spring air, making her glad she'd worn one of her old Tulane sweatshirts tonight. Balancing herself on the narrow seat, she leaned forward to retie one of her plain white sneakers.

"According to Hildy, business dinners are about all you ever have these days," Remy continued.

So what if she did, Jill thought, incensed. If she wanted a life that was all work and no play, that was her business. "And I suppose you know all about marriage?" Jill said, deciding it was time the conversation went back to him again. She retied her other shoe, too, just for good measure.

"Nope," Remy said. "Never been married."

"Ah-ha!" Jill sat up straight. In the dusky light, his sandy hair looked even blonder, his brown eyes darker.

"I have been engaged," Remy continued.

Jill studied the sun-blushed lines of his angular face. If he was still feeling hurt over the breakup, he was hiding it well. "What happened?" she asked, then thought of the way he'd come on to her, the way Carole Destrehan still seemed to be lusting after Remy although they were apparently no longer dating. She wondered if Remy was fickle. "Did you back out?" She knew she was prying; she didn't care.

"Not because I wanted it that way," Remy said. "I was engaged to a career woman who could never find the right time to be married. After about three years of the runaround, I broke it off."

Another heartbeat of silence followed. "You seem okay with it now," Jill observed as an intermittent drizzle began to fall.

He shrugged. *"Lâchez pas la patate."*

"Which means . . . ?"

" 'Don't let go of the potato.' You gotta hang in there, no matter what, and not let things that happen destroy you."

"Glib advice," Jill said as she thought about the empty, shell-shocked way she had felt at the time of her divorce.

"Stuff happens to everyone, Jill," Remy said softly, his eyes shining with a new compassionate light. "Besides, I think whatever happens is usually for the best in the long run."

Jill studied his contented expression as they rounded another bend in the swamp. The only sound, besides the occasional call of a bird or flutter of wings, was the water lapping gently against the side of the boat as they moved smoothly through the channel. "You really believe that?"

Abruptly, he broke into a mischievous grin. "Yeah, I do, 'cause if I hadn't broken up with Marilyn, I wouldn't be here with you now, fighting Kizzie's Love Potion #5 with all my might. But back to your story,

Jill. What happened to make you end your marriage?''

It was none of Remy's business. She didn't have to tell him. But if she didn't, he'd probably just go back and ask her aunt. Jill met his glance. She expected him to be looking for another way to make fun of her, or come on to her, but he wasn't. All she saw in his eyes was understanding and the need to know her better. Well, maybe if he did, he would understand why she wasn't in the market for a new romance, and would back off.

"I fell in love with an actor on 'As The World Spins' when I first moved to New York. I was a staff writer on the show and Jake was the young soap opera heartthrob of the moment. By the time we had been married five years, we had both achieved astonishing success. I was up for the head writer position on 'The Brave and the Beautiful.' He was offered the lead of a prime-time action-adventure show on another network. The problem was, my promotion was in New York and his was in Los Angeles. He wanted me to go, but I couldn't. I suggested we try a bicoastal marriage. He said no. Either I went with him or the marriage was over. I thought he would change his mind when he cooled down, but he didn't. A few weeks after he arrived in Los Angeles, he moved in with another actress, I was served with divorce papers and that was it.''

Remy frowned. "So Hildy was right. You were devastated."

It had felt as though someone had reached in and ripped out her heart. It had hurt far more than her father's gradual desertion of her, years prior to that. And the experience had left her unable to trust anyone ever again. Not wanting Remy to know that, for fear he'd bestow her with even more Cajun folk wisdom, Jill shrugged her shoulders as if her divorce had been just a passing blip on the computer screen of her life.

Ever so casually, Jill admitted, "Yes, I was hurt because Jake deserted me, and disillusioned because I had thought our love was strong enough to handle anything and it wasn't, but I picked myself up pretty rapidly and went on."

Did you now? Remy's look said. He dug his paddle into the water with more than necessary force, moving them faster and faster along. "Jake didn't love you," Remy announced grimly as he guided them past a beaver dam and a deep, dark pond. "If he had, he would have accepted you on any terms, and he would have considered your right to a happy life and fulfilling career just as important as his right to both."

"How can you say that when you left your fiancée because her career was important to her?" Jill said. The drizzling rain stopped, and still, cool air closed around them.

"I didn't break the engagement because she had a career. I broke it because she refused to be honest with herself, and with me, about what she really wanted. Marilyn said she wanted to marry me, to settle down and have a family while she continued working, but the reality was, she just didn't want to face the fact that that wasn't what she wanted at all, and so she kept looking for little excuses…little delays…anything to put off having to admit to herself that she just didn't love me enough to make that kind of lifelong commitment to me. That's what I resent."

Jill shook her head. Remy had bounced back from his disappointment in love much better than she had; she envied him his resiliency, even as she doubted his abruptly understanding manner. "You seem awfully enlightened."

He quirked a sandy brow. Intelligence radiated from his dark brown eyes. "And that surprises you?"

"Yes," Jill admitted with a frank look. "Not that it matters to me whether you're enlightened or understanding at all," Jill explained, lifting a hand from the side of the boat long enough to smooth her hair. "I have no intention of ever getting involved with anyone again."

"Is that so?"

"Yes," Jill said flatly, meaning it. "I'm married to my career now." And her career had never disappointed her.

Remy made a face. "Now that is a shame, sugar. A beautiful woman like you ought to have romance in her life, and plenty of it."

"I'll take my romance vicariously, through the soaps, thank you very much."

Remy grinned and brought the pirogue up to the edge of the wooden dock. "Vicarious romance can't begin to compete with the real thing," he said, securing the pirogue to the dock with a rope. Finished, he stepped out of the boat and gave Jill a hand up. Her legs were a little wobbly after sitting in the boat for such a long time. She held on to his hand tightly. He slid a hand around her waist to steady her, and looked down at her, all easy sensual grace. Jill's throat was suddenly very dry. Without warning, his mouth was very near, very soft and very appealing in an unutterably masculine way. She didn't have to think very hard to recall how giving and tender that mouth of his could be, or remember just how warm and sensuous and right his lips had felt when he had kissed her... *really* kissed her....

"What next?" Jill said, more anxious than ever to get the antidote.

"See that shack up over there?" he said, pointing to a house on stilts some hundred yards away. Jill nodded. "That's where we'll find my friend, Gator."

Hand cupping her elbow, Remy guided her past the alligator skins drying on the clothesline out in front of the shack and up to the front porch. Jill noted he was scanning the ground as he moved—probably for snakes. Staying close to him, she did the same.

An old man in a straw hat, overalls and a white T-shirt stepped out onto the porch. His skin was a sun-parched brown, his eyes light blue and friendly as could be. "Hey, Remy." Gator greeted his old friend with a lazy wave of his hand. He nodded at Jill. "This the gal you're determined to fall out of love with, the one you told me about on the shortwave radio?"

"The one and only," Remy drawled complacently as they followed Gator inside the house.

Jill was relieved to note it was very clean, if sparsely furnished.

"You all want to stay for dinner? Got some alligator sausage cooking on the stove," Gator said.

Jill's stomach rolled at the thought of eating alligator anything, but she smiled, appreciating the offer anyway. Without looking at Remy to see what he wanted to do, she said, "Thank you, but we've really got to be getting back. We're just going to have to take the potion and run, so to speak."

Gator grinned at her, then looked at Remy and said, "She's in a hurry to have the love magic removed, eh?"

"A big hurry," Jill confirmed, her patience fading slightly as she shifted her weight from foot to foot. "So, if we could just speed this up a little—"

Gator and Remy exchanged a man-to-man glance. Both looked slightly amused.

"Sure." Remy pulled a folded bill from his pocket.

Gator waved it away. "This is on me, my friend." He went to the cupboard and brought down two sparkling clean glasses that looked as though they'd once been jelly jars. He filled them with a dark brown liquid that smelled like raw whiskey when Jill lifted her glass to her face. She looked at Remy, then at Gator, then back at Remy again. She lowered her glass to her waist. "Are you sure this is going to work?"

Remy shrugged. "Only one way to find out." He tipped his glass and downed it, then wiped his mouth with the back of his hand.

Jill knew she was only doing this for everyone else. She didn't believe in love potions, Cajun or otherwise, but Remy, her aunt and Kizzie all apparently did, and it was important that they all believe the spell was broken. She lifted her glass to her face once again. The vapor from the dark brown liquid was almost overwhelming, but she forced herself to drain her glass in one swallow, just as Remy had. And she'd thought Kizzie's potion was bad! It was a minute before she could stop coughing and fighting for breath, another before she could stop grimacing.

Remy and Gator grinned from ear to ear. "A little strong for you, pretty lady?" Gator teased.

"And then some," Jill wheezed hoarsely. "What was in that?" She held up a hand before he could answer. "On second thought, I don't want to know."

"Thank you, my friend," Remy said. He shook hands with Gator before heading out the door.

"Sure you don't want to stay for supper?" Gator asked again, his light blue eyes twinkling as he walked them out to the boat.

"Thanks, but we better get back. I have a feeling Jill's not going to like being out in the swamp after dark," Remy said.

Remy was right about that, Jill thought as she settled back into the pirogue. The sky was already a dusky gray blue. She figured they had fifteen minutes of dusk left at best; then it would be pitch black, with only Remy's lantern and the light of the moon to show the way back to his place, and the safety of his pickup truck. What if they got lost? There were no street signs out here, only strands of watermarked cypress trees, old stumps and beaver dams to show the way.

Seeing the alligators and snakes in the daylight was one thing. After dark ... She shuddered, knowing she wouldn't rest until she got back on dry land again, and away from the swamp and all the reptiles that inhabited it.

"What's the matter?" Remy said as he climbed down into the pirogue after her, picked up his oar and untied the rope from the dock.

"I can't believe I'm actually here, in a swamp, taking love potions from someone I barely know," Jill moaned as soon as they were out of earshot. "And it's all Kizzie's fault."

"Oh, I don't know about that," Remy drawled as he turned the pirogue around in the direction they'd come. "I think you had some hand in what happened."

Jill's head was spinning. She told herself her sudden light-headedness was from the change in direction, and had nothing whatsoever to do with the raw whiskey she'd just downed so quickly. "What do you mean?" Jill retorted indignantly as she pressed a hand to her forehead, hoping a little discretionary pressure there would stop the reeling. "I've tried my best with Kizzie! She's the one who won't cooperate with me, won't keep regular hours!" Jill gripped the edges of the boat on either side of her and tried to focus on Remy, who looked a little out of focus as he paused to light the lantern.

"She can't help that. She has to be available to help her husband bring in the crawfish nets."

Jill kept a hold on the edges of the boat. She discovered Remy came back into focus if she squinted.

Oblivious to the fact she was feeling more than a little tipsy, Remy continued conversationally as he drove the paddle into the water with smooth rhythmic motions of his arms. "Used to be, crawfish fisherman could make a damn good livelihood. But these days, crawfish sell for twenty dollars a bag, and people like Kizzie and her husband are competing with the crawfish and alligator farms that have sprung up all over the place. Nowadays, they have to work a lot harder for a lot less. In addition to wanting to put her kids through school, that's why Kizzie started working for your aunt Hildy in the first place, 'cause they could no longer make a go of it just fishing the swamp.''

''How do you know all this?'' Jill let go of the boat, then grasped it quickly again when dizziness hit her in undulating waves. Her tongue felt as if it were coated with molasses. Her vision was fuzzy at best. Too late, she knew she never should have drunk that potion.

'''Cause I know Kizzie.'' Remy squinted at her. ''Say, you feeling okay?'' He apparently was, Jill thought resentfully.

Come to think of it, Jill did feel pretty smashed, but not about to let him know that, she said, ''Of course.'' She tried to sit up straight to prove it, but strangely, suddenly seemed unable to find her balance. With a muttered oath, she lurched clumsily to the left, and almost tumbled headfirst out of the side of the boat.

Remy swore and secured his pole to the side of the boat. The next thing Jill knew he was twisting her around so they no longer faced each other. One arm anchored securely around her waist, he pulled her back so she was situated between his legs. ''Guess what, Remy?'' Jill said with a giggle she knew was inappropriate but seemed unable to quell. ''I think that potion of Gator's was 'bout two hundred proof.''

"You know what? I think you're right." Remy tightened his hand protectively around her waist, and drew her back against the solid warmth of his chest and into the intimate cradle of his muscular thighs. "When was the last time you ate something?" he asked, his warm breath stirring her hair, his voice low and protective.

"I dunno." Jill sighed, and luxuriated in the feeling of being held so closely against him. "Maybe about lunchtime." She frowned, thinking. Had she had lunch or had she worked straight through it? "Maybe not." She licked her lips sensuously.

Remy groaned. "Great. A tipsy woman in a pirogue. Just what I need."

It felt so warm and cozy and nice being held against Remy like this, Jill thought to herself. Whoever would have guessed that would be the case? Not her! "Well, at least Kizzie's potion has been canceled out," Jill said around a yawn. Now that she was in Remy's strong warm arms, she felt much better. And a little sleepy, too.

"Speak for yourself, sugar," Remy murmured beneath his breath, shifting his weight slightly behind her.

"Oh, not to worry, Remy," Jill continued airily, "nothing's going to happen."

"*I* know that," he said. Then peered down at her, still holding her with one arm, and maneuvering the oar with the other. "The question is, do you?"

"Very funny," Jill said.

Remy let go of her, still holding her safely between his thighs, and used both powerful arms to guide the pirogue toward his fishing shack. When the bow hit the muddy shoreline, he let go of her completely and got out. Ashore, he reached over and grasped her hand. "Think you can stand?" he said, peering at her with real concern.

"Of course I can stand," Jill said, smoothing the hem of her sweatshirt primly. The only problem was, her legs didn't seem to work, and neither did the rest of her. She tried once, and then again, but the funny thing was, her body didn't seem to move.

Remy watched the whole process, then groaned and swore again. "I knew I should've asked if you'd had something to eat before you took the potion, sugar," he said.

Jill smiled up at him. "How come most of these potions end up being alcohol-based?" she said as he slid a hand beneath her knees and picked her up. "And how come you're not affected?"

"'Cause I weigh twice as much as you do and I had three square meals today." With Jill cradled in his arms, he strode over the muddy ground and up the dozen steps to the wooden shack on stilts.

"Now what?" Jill said.

"Now we get some food into you," Remy said as he unlocked the door. He set her down just inside.

The room was spinning like a top, and so was her heart, but Remy was solid as a rock. Jill slipped her arms around his neck and held on tight. "Remy," she murmured sexily, "make it stop."

"Oh, God, Jill," he groaned. "Don't do this to me."

"Come on," she whispered throatily as her inhibitions slid away, one by precious one. "I just wanna test the antidote." She just wanted to see what one of his kisses would feel like when the world was already spinning.

"No testing," Remy said sternly, looking abruptly like a school principal reprimanding a rowdy class. Hands on her waist, he danced her backward to a wooden chair and guided her down into it. "Sit here, while I cook."

Jill meant to do as he said; she really did.

But as she watched him move about the small metal cookstove, all she could think about was how handsome he looked, and how his arms had felt around her, so right and so gentle. He wanted her, antidote or no antidote. And right now, she wanted him. She stood and made her way to his side. The way she was feeling right now, she doubted she would remember any of this in the morning, and she doubted he would, either. So what did she really have to lose? she wondered recklessly.

REMY HAD JUST OPENED the can of soup when he heard Jill get out of the chair he'd put her in.

Remy groaned.

He had hoped taking Jill out to see his friend, Gator Dupres, to drink an "antidote" would put an end to the love potion nonsense, once and for all. Instead, it had only made the situation that much worse.

Thanks to the high alcohol content of the potion, Jill's normal inhibitions had all but disappeared. Remy's hadn't. Worse, Jill was going to be mad as hell at him when the whiskey-laced antidote did wear off, which meant he was going to be in a heap of trouble.

Jill came to a halt just behind him. Remy sucked in a breath as she slipped her arms around his waist, and rested the side of her face against his back. "Whatcha doin'?" she asked thickly.

Remy ignored the way his lower body surged to life and hoped Jill wouldn't notice it, either. "Trying to fix you something to eat," he said.

She slipped around to face him, keeping her arms on his waist. Inserting her slender body between his and the counter, she tilted her head up and looked into his eyes. "I'm not hungry, Remy."

Remy was, but it wasn't food he craved. It was the sweet taste of her lips beneath his, the soft feel of her body pressed tightly against his. "Too bad, Jill, 'cause you need to eat something, and I'm here to see that you do," he said sternly.

He had brought her out to the swamp to take an antidote to clear the way, so they could have a romance, without superstition clouding their feelings. He wasn't going to let the abundance of whiskey in Gator's antidote negate that. He was determined to do the right thing here, no matter how hard she made it for him.

Putting his hands on her waist, he lifted her up off the floor and over a half foot or so to his left. "Now if you'll give me a little room, I'll get your soup ready."

She grinned like a mischievous little girl and darted back to where she'd been. She unbuttoned the top two buttons of his shirt and slipped her hand inside, against his skin, caressing softly, wantonly. "I don't want to give you some room, Remy. I want you so close, you don't know what to do." She looped her free arm around his neck and flashed him a naughty grin.

Remy sighed as she continued caressing his chest. God knew he had never been one to turn away from the prospect of pleasure, but Jill would regret this in the morning, or as soon as that potion had worn off. And when that happened, she was going to be mad as hell at him. As much as he wanted to take her into his arms and into his bed, he knew he couldn't take advantage of her. "Sugar, you're driving me nuts," he warned. Remy scooped Jill up in his arms and carried her over to his bed and dropped her down in the center of it.

Jill grasped his shirt and pulled him down with her. It was either have his shirt ripped or go with the flow. Remy chose the latter and landed on top of her. Damn, she was asking for trouble, he thought. And the trouble was, if she were even half-sober, she wouldn't be behaving this way at all. Remy knew that. "Time for a test, sugar," Jill drawled tipsily.

Lacing her arms around his neck, she pulled his head down to hers. Remy knew what she wanted. What could one kiss hurt? "Now, let's jus' see if that antidote worked," Jill said.

Her lips touched his. Remy groaned and held back. She deepened the kiss. Caught up in the moment, he buried his hands in her hair and kissed her back, once, twice, until he ached with the need to possess her, heart and soul. But when her fingers went to unfasten the rest of the buttons on his shirt, he knew he had to stop—now.

The consequences of her hating him were too much to bear.

With a groan, he broke off the kiss and rolled onto his back. Breathing heavily, he stared at the ceiling of the fishing shack. A drunken roll in the hay was not what he wanted. Jill deserved better. Hell, they both did.

Silence fell between them. Jill's breath came erratically. Her face was white and pink simultaneously. He knew the whiskey had done all the damage it was going to do. Jill was starting to sober up.

"I've shocked you," she said, after a moment, sounding, if possible, even more miserable than he felt. "Well, not to worry, I've shocked myself." She sat up on the side of the bed and buried her head in her hands. Her moan was low, distressed, and considering what had almost happened between them, Remy thought, perfectly understandable. "I don't know what's gotten into me," she said.

Remy did. "Nothing to be embarrassed about, sugar. What we felt just now is perfectly natural. In fact, it was probably inevitable from the first moment we met."

She sat up straight and glared at him. "I'm sure you think so! This probably happens to you all the time. It's never happened to me before in my life!" She bolted for his bathroom.

He charged after her and stood in the doorway while she splashed cold water on her face. Wordlessly, he handed her a towel.

"It had to be that damn antidote." She stormed past him. "If there hadn't been something in that... something vile...then I never, *never* would have done what I just did!"

"Sugar, that antidote had quite a bit of alcohol in it," Remy said reasonably, not surprised that Jill would be looking for any reason, save her own desire for him and his for her, to explain what had just happened between them. But that's all it was...chemistry...causing them both to act this way.

Jill shook her head vigorously, stubbornly refusing to own up to their passion. "I've accidentally had too much to drink before, Remy. I still didn't grab my date and try to pull his clothes off." She tightened her hands into fists and glared at him determinedly. "I want you to find out exactly what was in that antidote!"

Remy noticed the soup was very close to boiling dry and walked over to turn off the stove. "Now?"

"Yes, now!" Jill demanded emotionally. "This instant!"

Remy realized it was either humor her or have an hysterical woman on his hands. With a shrug, he started for the shortwave radio he kept on hand for emergencies. It took a moment, but he finally got Gator to answer his SOS. "Gator, my friend, I've got an upset lady friend here."

There was a chuckle on the other end. A mischievous chuckle. Remy groaned. No, he thought. No, tell me you didn't play a prank, he thought. Ignoring the way Jill had her arms folded, Remy asked, "What exactly was in that antidote you gave Jill and me, Gator?''

"Besides the tincture, you mean?" Gator asked.

Jill tugged on Remy's sleeve. "What's a tincture?" she interrupted.

"A base solution of alcohol and water," Remy said in an aside to her. "Beside the tincture, Gator, what was in the potion?"

"Oh, many wonderful, magical things, my friend. A handful of rosemary leaves, thirteen anise seeds, four cloves, a tablespoon of honey and a smidgen of elderberry wine. Plus a slight amount of jimson weed and foxglove," Gator Dupres said, and began to laugh as if he had just played a very big joke on Remy.

And he had. "I owe you for this one, Gator," Remy said, then turned off the shortwave.

Jill looked at Remy impatiently, waiting for an explanation.

Remy didn't want to tell her, but he knew she could find out the meaning of the ingredients if she wanted to, so she might as well hear it from him first. "All those herbs are known for their aphrodisiac qualities," Remy said with a beleaguered sigh. They hadn't been given an antidote to a love potion. They'd been given another Cajun folk magic aphrodisiac on top of the first.

It took less than a moment for the impact of his words to sink in. "Are you telling me we were double-crossed?" Jill demanded. It was a small relief to Jill that Remy looked no happier about the turn of events than she did. He nodded reluctantly. "How long is this second aphrodisiac supposed to last?'' she demanded.

"Beats me," Remy said with a grimace. If he were to judge from the way he was feeling now, it would be quite a while.

They both muttered their displeasure simultaneously, his in Cajun French, hers in blatant English. Their eyes met.

Remy couldn't believe superstition and love potions were once again interfering with the development of their romance. It wasn't supposed to work this way. He was darn sure Kizzie and Hildy and even Gator hadn't intended to squelch any passion Jill might have felt for him. But they had!

"I can't live like this," Jill said, meaning it.

Now that she was relatively sober again, she couldn't believe she had made such a fool of herself, throwing herself at Remy that way. So he was handsome and sexy in a devil-may-care way. Did that mean she had to come on to him like gangbusters and try to seduce him into bed? Potion or no potion, antidote or no antidote, she knew better. And so did he!

"Hey," Remy said, catching her accusing glance as he jabbed a thumb at his sternum. "This has not been a picnic for me, either! I didn't ask for this!"

He hadn't complained when he was kissing her, Jill thought.

"Well, we have to do something about it!" Jill said, folding her arms in front of her defiantly. The question was . . . what?

Chapter Six

"You poor darlings," Hildy said from her hospital bed the next morning, after their story had been recounted—right up to the moment when Jill had tried to seduce Remy. That part, Jill had no intention of telling anyone. It was enough for them to tell her aunt she and Remy were feeling strangely attracted to one another, and that they wanted to deep-six said attraction.

She wanted a life that revolved around her work. Remy had said he wanted a woman who would and could get married now, a woman who would settle down and give him a family. While the idea of a husband and children appealed to Jill, she wasn't ready to make that kind of commitment again. She was afraid if she did, she'd end up getting hurt and disillusioned again. And that, she knew, she couldn't bear.

"Are you all right now?" Hildy asked, looking from Jill to Remy.

"Of course we're all right," Jill said softly, her face heating with a telltale blush. She was just frustrated, that was all . . . having gone to all the trouble to go out into the swamp to get an antidote, only to find out it

wasn't an antidote they'd taken after all, but an aphrodisiac. Jill scooted her chair closer to Hildy's hospital bed. "The problem is, Aunt Hildy, we don't
know what to do next. Just ignore everything and
hope that'll be the end of it...."

Remy gave Jill a look that let her know he recalled
every second of their clinch on his bed the evening before. He bent forward and whispered in her ear, so
only she could hear. "I wouldn't count on that."

Jill paused to cast Remy a censuring look, then
turned back to her aunt. "Or I was hoping... Maybe
if you talked to Kizzie for us, Aunt Hildy, that—"

Aunt Hildy shook her head, vetoing the idea before Jill could even finish getting the words out.
"Kizzie won't take a love spell off until she is good and
ready, and it would seem, from everything she told me
last night when she visited, that she thinks the two of
you are a match made in Cajun heaven."

"I'm not Cajun," Jill said, blushing all the more,
"and neither are you, Aunt Hildy."

"Yes, but Remy is."

They both turned to look at Remy. For once, he was
almost serious. "If I were to get romantically involved with Jill, I wouldn't want it to be because of
any love potion we took."

Then what reason would he consider acceptable? Jill
wondered. Love? With a start, she stopped that
thought as soon as it occurred. She was not going to
permit herself to fantasize about her aunt's Cajun
neighbor, even if he was one of the sexiest, most fun-
loving men she had ever met.

"Remy, we have to be practical here. You and I live in different parts of the country. I am only going to be in Louisiana a few more days."

"Details, details," Remy said.

"My life revolves around my work. I have time for Aunt Hildy but little more," Jill said flatly.

"Now, that *is* a shame," Remy said sincerely.

"I agree," Hildy said. She looked at Jill. "You are throwing away a wonderful opportunity here, honey."

"Be that as it may," Jill retorted, "it's my decision to make!"

Avoiding Jill's glance altogether, Remy paused thoughtfully. If he was hurt by her refusal to get further romantically involved with him, Jill thought, he wasn't showing it.

"Any ideas on what we should do next, Hildy?" Remy asked.

"Yes. First I think you should both stop fretting about the love potion so much," Hildy advised.

"Easier said than done," Jill muttered cantankerously. Every time she had closed her eyes the previous night and tried to sleep, she had remembered leaning back against Remy's chest in the pirogue, coming on to him in the fishing shack, the way he'd kissed her, and almost…almost let her undress him. Whether she wanted to admit it or not, there was something inexplicably powerful and erotic between them, something unlike anything she had ever experienced. Remy knew it and felt it, too.

"Well, try harder," Hildy advised Jill. "Because the garden club is coming out to Magnolia Place on Saturday, and so far we've made no preparations at all."

Jill opened her handbag and took out her leather appointment book and pen. "What do you want me to do?" Jill asked. She didn't want her aunt fretting about anything. And she knew how Hildy tended to fret before hosting any event.

Hildy smiled. "I want you and Remy to drive into New Orleans this morning and stop by Laura's Original Praline and Fudge Shoppe and buy pralines, hand-dipped chocolates and rum-flavored pecans for the party. Then go by Yvonne LeFleur's—I have a dress there, waiting to be picked up, and she's going to wonder what's happened to me! I'd also like some fresh potpourri. You can use your judgment about where to buy that, Jill, and some new scented candles, lace doilies . . . and what do you think about centerpieces for the tables?"

"I'll find something," Jill promised.

"And then take Remy to lunch at Arnaud's," Hildy finished. "He's done so much for me. Since he won't let me pay him in cash, we'll just have to do it in good old Southern hospitality."

"I KNOW WHAT your aunt Hildy said, but you don't have to take me to lunch," Remy said several hours later after he and Jill had almost completed their list of errands. *Particularly since you are so determined not to get involved with me,* he thought.

"Sure I do," Jill said, as they followed the formally dressed waiter across the polished mosaic-tiled floor to a table in Arnaud's large turn-of-the-century dining room.

Remy held her chair. "Why?"

Finding it far too disturbing to look into Remy's knowing dark brown eyes for any length of time, for fear he would see that the attraction she felt for him was growing by leaps and bounds with every second they spent together, Jill looked out one of the beveled glass windows. "Because I promised my aunt. Besides—" she turned back to give Remy a flip look "—I'm hungry, the food here is fabulous and it's been at least two years since I've dined here."

Remy gave her a look of mock astonishment. Half his mouth crooked up in a teasing smile. "So this is Southern hospitality at its genteel best," he quipped dryly, laying his napkin across his lap.

Jill fingered the sterling silver next to her plate and focused on the crystal chandelier overhead. "Aunt Hildy knows not what she asks," Jill muttered under her breath.

"Actually, I think your aunt knows exactly what she asks," Remy said, perusing the menu. "I think she's matchmaking, too, right along with Kizzie and Gator. In the sweetest possible way, of course."

Jill looked up from her menu and studied him bluntly. "And that doesn't bother you, does it?" She would have expected Remy to be as exasperated with Kizzie and Hildy and Gator as she was. Instead, he seemed to be taking the matchmaking machinations of the disparate group in stride.

"Not nearly as much as what happened last night bothers me," he admitted frankly.

They were silent a minute, recalling. "I still don't believe in love potions," Jill said after they had placed their orders.

"Neither do I," Remy admitted. "And yet...you and I both admitted last night that we'd never behaved quite so recklessly before. I mean, I knew Gator's potion had knocked you for a loop, and I ended up on the bed with you anyway. That's not like me. I have not ever taken advantage of a woman who's had too much to drink, Jill. And yet last night when you grabbed my shirt and looked up at me like that, all soft and womanly and yearning, I— Well, I'm embarrassed to say I forgot myself for a moment."

They both had, Jill thought ruefully. And though she wanted to blame it all on the potion and the alcohol-based aphrodisiac, she knew her own feelings, and maybe his, too, had come into play, at least a little bit. They had to deal with these feelings and make sure they didn't surface again. Because she didn't want to be loved and left again. For that, she knew only one solution. And that was to talk her way out of this mess...even if what she had to say was all more or less psychobabble.

"It's obvious what has happened here, Remy," Jill said, with the cool reasoned approach of a professor lecturing a class. "Kizzie and Gator have tapped into all our deep-rooted innate superstitions and made us extra sensitive to each other's thoughts and feelings and body language, to the point where we're projecting latent desires where there are none. And our powerful imaginations and subconsciousnesses are picking up where those mental projections leave off, and it's all working to make us think—on a very primitive level, mind you—that we're under some kind of a spell. And obviously, that's why we're doing what we're doing, and behaving the way we're behaving.''

Remy gave her a level look over the rim of his water glass. ''If you say so.''

Jill speared another piece of lettuce with her fork and leaned toward him, aggrieved. ''Don't tell me you really believe in all this bunk.''

Remy frowned and set his glass down. ''To tell you the truth, Jill, I didn't. But last night when we got back to the shack, all I had on my mind was fixing you something to eat, sobering you up and getting you out of there as soon as was humanly possible. And yet the minute you touched me . . . the minute you started kissing me . . .'' He shook his head in silent regret. ''I don't know what happened. One minute I was in control, the next I nearly lost it . . . and like I said earlier, that has never happened to me before. Which, in turn, made me wonder if maybe the two of us aren't destined to have a romance.''

''The only thing the two of us are destined to do is get out of this matchmaking mess with our sanity intact,'' Jill grumbled as she finished her salad and pushed the plate away. ''Furthermore, if you got carried away inexplicably last night, it was for the same reason I did, because of the aphrodisiac Gator gave you,'' she said.

Remy shook his head. ''I've had so-called aphrodisiacs before, Jill. We used to fool around with them in college. They never worked. Not like that.''

Jill fingered the sterling-silver spoon to the right of her plate. She had no experience with aphrodisiacs. She had to bow to his expertise here. ''Well, maybe when you were in college you just didn't have the right dose.''

"And maybe," Remy said with a pointed look in her direction as teasing lights leapt into his eyes, "there's more to Kizzie's magic potion than either of us wants to admit. Maybe we ought to stop fighting our feelings and just go with the flow."

If she did that, Jill thought, she'd be in Remy's bed in no time flat. Fortunately, for both of them, she was much more sensible than that. She was not going to start an affair that would end up disappointing them both. "You're talking nonsense again," Jill said. The waiter returned to clear their salad plates and put shrimp Arnaud in front of Remy and trout meunière in front of her.

Remy shrugged and dug into his shrimp. "I might agree that we should just shrug off the love potion Kizzie gave us if we hadn't already experienced the fireworks between us, but we did. And there's something else that occurred to me this morning. Kizzie isn't just known for her love potions. She makes a lot of folk medicine and herbal cures, as well, all of which have been proven to be very effective. So, if her folk medicines work to cure people, who says her love potions can't make people fall in love?"

Goose bumps rose on Jill's arms; she attributed them to the ceiling fans whirling softly overhead, rather than Remy's sexy drawl. "Kizzie knows how to use herbs to cure people?" Jill asked. Her aunt hadn't said anything about that!

Remy nodded authoritatively. "She's got salves for rashes and sunburn, poultices for arthritis, homemade decongestants for coughs."

"And they work?"

"Ninety-nine percent of the time." Remy studied Jill, his desire to continue to spend time with her evident. "Look, as long as we're here . . . there are lots of shops in the French Quarter that specialize in removing charms and spells." He smiled at her as if issuing a dare. "What do you say we go into a few of them and see if we can't find a real antidote for the double dose of love potion we took?"

JILL DIDN'T BELIEVE for a moment that any antidote was going to erase the chemistry she felt for Remy. It was just too strong. But if it worked to convince Remy and Kizzie and her aunt that she was serious about not having a romance with him, then the effort would have been well worth it. So an hour later, after they had finished their meal at Arnaud's, they left the restaurant, strolled the Quarter and finally selected a shop on Bourbon Street that advertised Love Potions and Charms in the window.

No sooner had they stepped inside the dark musty interior of the shop, than Jill began to have second thoughts. "I don't know about this, Remy." Jill stood on tiptoe and whispered into his ear, "There's a lot of voodoo stuff in here and I don't like it." Jill cast her glance away from a display of tom-toms and scary-looking masks. "It gives me the creeps."

Remy looked at the chicken claws and feathers hanging from the ceiling, and back at the brown bottles on display in the pharmaceutical case. "You've got a point there, sugar." Wrapping an arm about her waist, he guided her away from a cageful of snakes. "Maybe this isn't where we should be looking for a cure."

Jill grabbed his wrist and pulled him back out into the sunshine of the street. Realizing she was trembling, she stuffed her hand back into her pocket. "At least Kizzie's magic is the good, old-fashioned folksy kind," Jill said.

"And you want to stick to that?"

"Don't you?"

He nodded.

"So now what?" Jill looked at Remy and waited.

He rubbed a hand along the underside of his jaw. "Well, I've never been there but I've heard of a gift shop in La Place called Madame Rousseau's that also does some back room love-charm business. The lady who runs it has a reputation for making potions to keep errant husbands and lovers in line."

"But we don't want a love potion," Jill said in exasperation. "We want an antidote to one."

Remy lifted his hands, looking as much at a loss about what to do as she felt. "Well, it wouldn't hurt to ask, would it?" he said.

"I guess not," Jill allowed slowly, running her fingers through her cloud of dark hair. Especially if it showed Remy how determined she was not to get involved with him. Unfortunately, doing so would mean spending even more time with each other, and she wasn't so sure that was a good idea. The more they were together, the stronger their innate chemistry seemed to get.

"You want to stop by on the way back to Magnolia Place?" Remy asked. His hand on her shoulders, he guided her in the direction of his pickup truck. "It's about halfway between here and there."

Jill shrugged and tried not to notice how her shoulder tingled where he touched her. "At this point, what do we have to lose?"

To Jill's surprise, the shop Remy had in mind was located in a small, neatly kept cottage with pink gingerbread trim. White lace curtains adorned the windows. Inside were shelves of knickknacks, stuffed animals, dried flowers and potpourri. The proprietress was an attractive woman in her late fifties, dressed in a long flowing gown of indigo blue. She wore a matching turban on her head and large gold earrings. "How may I help you two lovebirds?" Madame Rousseau asked.

Too late, Jill realized she and Remy were standing so close together they looked like a couple. Knowing that was an impression she didn't want to give, she moved away from him decisively. "We're not lovebirds," she said.

Remy grinned at Jill and stuck a hand in the back pocket of his jeans. "I understand you know a lot about love potions, Madame Rousseau. Do you also know a lot about antidotes for them?"

"But of course, darlings!" Madame Rousseau waved them toward the back room. She gestured for them to sit down at the table in the center of the room. Jill caught a glimpse of the crystal ball in the corner and rolled her eyes. She was not falling victim to superstition here. Remy chastised her with a look.

"Sit down, darlings, and tell Madame Rousseau all about it. Why is it you took a love potion and why do you now want it reversed?"

Reminding herself she was doing this to dissuade Remy, Jill sat down reluctantly. Remy drew a chair up beside her. Briefly, he covered the story of Kizzie's potion, and then Gator's, and the ingredients he suspected had been in each potion. As with her aunt Hildy, he left out all information about the kisses he and Jill had shared. But to Jill's chagrin, Madame Rousseau seemed to guess about those kisses anyway.

"And these potions have made the two of you feel intense desire for each other, yes?" Madame said.

Remy nodded as Jill struggled not to feel so silly and self-conscious. "So," Remy said, leaning back in his chair and looking perfectly at ease, "what have you got that will nullify the effects of the stuff we've already ingested?"

Madame held up a cautionary hand. Her expression was solemn. "It will not be inexpensive," she warned.

"Remy and I are not paying more than twenty dollars, no matter what you put in it," Jill interrupted.

Madame hesitated. "All right," she said finally, disappearing into yet another back room. "I'll see what I can do."

It took a good five minutes. Finally, Madame returned with two cups of tea and a mysterious brown vial. "Is there alcohol in this?" Jill asked suspiciously.

Madame shook her head. "Not a drop."

Jill looked at Remy, recalling what had happened the last time she'd been gullible enough to drink an antidote. Even if this would work on him psychologically, she suddenly wasn't so sure she wanted to participate.

"The tincture in this potion is peppermint tea," Madame reassured.

Remy held out a hand anyway. "Mind if I sample what's in the vial?"

Madame reluctantly gestured her approval. Remy sniffed, then put a dab on his fingertip and tasted a drop. "Definitely not alcoholic," he said.

Beside him, Jill breathed a silent sigh of relief.

Madame added a dash of dark brown liquid to each cup of tea. Jill and Remy lifted their cups. "You're sure this is going to work?" Jill said. Anything to make Remy stop chasing her. Anything to make her stop yearning to get caught.

Madame Rousseau nodded firmly. "I promise you, darlings. This potion will definitely sour your love."

"YUCK!" JILL SAID five minutes later as the two of them returned to his pickup truck. She rummaged around in the bottom of her handbag for a breath mint. "That was the worst-tasting tea I've ever had in my life."

"I agree," Remy said. In fact, he had known it was going to be bad when he had tasted a drop of what was in the brown bottle. But what the hell. If he was in for a penny, he might as well be in for a pound. Besides, if going through all this rigamarole made Jill feel that

Kizzie's Cajun love spell was off of them, Gator's aphrodisiac completely negated, and that whatever passion was left between them was of one hundred percent natural origin, then drinking the noxious antidote was well worth it.

He didn't want Jill thinking their attraction to each other was based on anything other than what he already knew it was: raw chemistry. And he had only to see the look on her face and watch her tremble when they'd entered the voodoo shop in the French Quarter to know how superstitious and suggestible a woman Jill was at heart. If bad magic or voodoo gave her the creeps, then good magic...or love potions...had to be having some effect on her, too.

He knew, of course, that she was hoping her keen interest in antidotes would dissuade him from pursuing her. Instead, the opposite was happening. The more time he spent with her, the more he wanted to make Jill his.

Oblivious to the nature of his thoughts, Jill handed Remy a peppermint Life Savers, and popped one in her mouth. "What do you think Madame Rousseau used to make that antidote taste so bad?" Jill asked.

Remy sucked on his mint. "Cider vinegar, or something very similar."

"That's what I thought, too." Jill screwed up her face comically as she fastened her seat belt. She groaned. "Yuck! I can't believe I just drank a whole cupful of vinegar-laced peppermint tea."

Me, either, Remy thought as he started the truck and backed it out onto the street. What a man wouldn't do to please a woman....

"Want to stop at that Sonic Drive-In up the street and get something cold to drink?" Jill asked.

"Absolutely," Remy said as they stopped at a red light. "Anything to get that taste out of my mouth."

As they waited for the light to change, Jill leaned back in her seat and shut her eyes. Her long dark lashes rested against the pale alabaster of her cheeks. Her lips were soft and bare, and to Remy's chagrin, looked imminently kissable despite the antidote they'd just imbibed. "Well, it worked anyway," Jill said with a sigh.

"What?" Remy asked, wishing he hadn't promised himself he wasn't going to take advantage of Jill again. Putting the moves on her when her eyes were shut fell under the heading of taking advantage.

"With this taste in my mouth, the last thing on my mind is kissing anyone," Jill said. "Ugh, ugh, ugh!"

Remy laughed softly as he guided his truck into the parking space, next to the speaker. He relaxed as he realized the antidote had done its job in convincing Jill that Kizzie's potion and Gator's aphrodisiac were now null and void. Unfortunately, it had done nothing to negate the desire he felt for Jill. He wanted to hold her and kiss her more than ever.

Telling himself to get his mind off kissing her again, because it just wasn't going to happen, not if Jill had any say in the matter, Remy studied the menu.

He knew he was putting off taking her back to Magnolia Place. It was inevitable they part again and go their own separate ways, but irrational as it was, he didn't want to let her go. He told himself it was the challenge Jill presented that kept him coming back time after time. He told himself his affection for Jill's aunt, the fact Hildy was in the hospital and was relying on him, was also making him feel protective of Jill, but even as he thought it, a part of him didn't buy it. He knew in his heart his interest in Jill went beyond his normal affinity for helping people. His interest in Jill was elemental, and of the man-woman variety.

"I know what I want. A large lemonade. How about you?"

"I'll have a cherry Coke."

"So what are your plans for the rest of the day?" Remy asked casually, once their drinks were delivered.

"After I stop by the hospital to see my aunt, I'll probably be up working most of the night on the story lines for next year."

Remy wondered if work was all Jill ever did. Hildy thought so. And from what he had seen, it certainly seemed to be true. "When is that due?" he asked.

"As soon as possible," Jill said, her dark blue eyes taking on a harried gleam. "Actually, I should have had it done last week, but there were some problems with one of the actors whose contract is up for renewal, and so I had to talk to him, and then I got behind. Then Aunt Hildy fell...and well, you know the rest. Since, it seems I've hardly been able to concentrate for more than a minute or two at a time. And every time I do start to concentrate, Kizzie walks in and scowls at me."

"Or I show up," Remy said, teasing her with a grin.

"Or you show up."

Their glances meshed. Jill's smile turned to shyness. Remy saw beneath all the attitude was a very vulnerable, very sensitive, very caring woman. "I'm sorry we got off on the wrong foot," Remy said.

"I am, too," Jill said. Again, they exchanged glances. And again, Remy found himself wishing they had a reason to spend more time together. A reason that would kick in today.

He wished he hadn't gone quite so far out of his way to provoke her just to get her attention the first day they had met. Remy paused. "About your work. Anything I can do to help?" He'd never been the domestic type, but suddenly he could see himself fetching pots of coffee and sandwiches for her while she worked. He could see himself giving her back rubs and making sure she took enough breaks, got enough sleep at night and was very thoroughly, very tenderly loved.

Jill shrugged in answer to his question of what he could do to help her. "Just get the electricity fixed."

Fixing the electricity meant not only helping Hildy out, it meant being close to Jill. "Will do, as soon as possible," Remy promised.

Chapter Seven

"C'mon, Hildy, they can't all be that bad," Remy said, after she had sent away the seventh applicant in two hours. They had all seemed like fine potential employees to him.

"Well, they are," Hildy grumbled as she sat in the chair next to her bed and laboriously answered a stack of get-well cards. "They look at me with pity, Remy. You may not see it, but I see it."

"Now you're beginning to sound like Jill," Remy teased. "I see where she gets her highly suspicious nature."

Hildy made a face at him and resumed writing. Remy grinned back and hunkered down beside her chair, so the two of them were face-to-face. "C'mon, talk to me, Hildy. Tell me what's really bothering you about all this, and it isn't the credentials or lack of them in any of the women you've interviewed so far."

Hildy released a sigh of irritation and put down her pen. "Well, if you must know, having a companion makes me feel like I need a baby-sitter. And I don't, Remy. So I fell once, when the lights went out unexpectedly. That doesn't mean it will ever happen again.''

Remy put his hand over Hildy's and gave it a comforting squeeze. ''I don't think your gracefulness is the problem here, Hildy. We're talking about your niece's peace of mind. Jill just wants to know that you are getting all the help you need during your recuperation, and since you don't want to return to New York with her—''

Hildy's face fell. ''I really don't want to live there, Remy.''

Remy gave Hildy's wrinkled hand another squeeze and got to his feet. He roamed the room restlessly, wishing he weren't in the middle of Hildy and Jill's differing views on this subject. Since he cared about Hildy, however, he figured he could play peacemaker this once. ''If you don't want to go back to New York with Jill, then so be it.''

''I knew you'd understand, Remy!'' Hildy cried.

Remy looked at Hildy sternly. ''But you also need to accept the fact that Jill has to do something that will enable her to go back to her job in New York with some peace of mind. Otherwise, she's not going to be able to go back.''

''Would that be so bad?'' Hildy cast him a sly look.

No, Remy thought, it wouldn't, if Jill were the least bit interested in him. Unfortunately, nine out of ten times Jill viewed him like an odious piece of trash that had washed up on the shores of Lake Pontchartrain. She desired him. She tolerated him. But she didn't want to do either.

Remy forced his mind back to the issue of hiring a companion to stay with Hildy at Magnolia Place. "C'mon, Hildy. You could do this for Jill, couldn't you?"

"I don't know, Remy. Having a complete stranger underfoot twenty-four hours a day . . ."

"Just for a month or two, until your arm is out of the cast and you've made a complete physical recovery."

Hildy motioned Remy toward the pitcher of ice water beside her bed. "You don't understand, Remy. At my age, giving up your independence, even briefly, is a serious thing." Hildy watched as Remy poured her a glass of water. "You often don't get it back. I don't want to start depending on someone else to do things for me that I could easily do for myself with a little effort and ingenuity."

Remy crossed the distance between them and handed Hildy her drink. "You will get your independence back, Hildy."

"How do you know?"

"Because I know you and I know your niece. Jill will give up eventually, but right now it is vitally important you humor her need to fuss over you."

"Well, I suppose you're right." Hildy took another sip of water and stared up at Remy thoughtfully. "We both know what a worrier Jill is. How she likes to be in charge of everything."

"Right, and—" The sudden scent of roses brought Remy's head up. Jill was standing in the doorway. She was dressed in a beige silk pantsuit that was sophisticated enough to wear to the best restaurant in New

Orleans. A long strand of pearls hung around her neck. She had a pretty smile on her face that didn't begin to reach her dark blue eyes. He knew, just by looking at her, that she had slept fitfully, if at all.

"Hello, Aunt Hildy," Jill said sweetly. She looked at him. "Remy, may I see you a moment—privately?" He nodded, wondering what was up. "We'll be right back, Aunt Hildy."

Jill led the way, her high heels *clicking* on the polished linoleum floor. The view from the back was as good as the view from the front, even if Jill was strung tighter than piano wire this morning.

She didn't look at him again until they reached the privacy of the sun porch, which thankfully, at that particular moment, was devoid of other visitors and patients. "You look upset," Remy remarked. He hoped she hadn't had bad news from Hildy's doctor.

"I am upset, Remy. If you must insert yourself into the middle of my family problems—and I must say I'm not sure why that is necessary now that I'm home—why can't you be more help in convincing my aunt that she needs to hire a companion?"

Working to hide his irritation, Remy walked over to the drink machine in the corner and inserted two quarters. He punched a button and a Dr Pepper can rolled out of the machine, landing with a thud in the bin at the bottom. "I was trying to help," Remy replied bluntly.

"Really," Jill said coolly. "It didn't sound that way to me."

Remy popped the tab on his drink can and took a long sip. Finished, he wiped his mouth with the back of his hand. "For your information, Jill, Hildy called me at seven this morning. She said the first of the companions was to arrive at 9:00 a.m., and she didn't feel up to interviewing them alone. Neither did she want to bother you, because she knew you were still writing next year's story line bible for 'The Brave and the Beautiful.' So I showed up here, with coffee and doughnuts, no less, and I sat through the first seven interviews. Your aunt did not like any of the potential companions Carole Destrehan sent."

Jill paced restlessly back and forth. She ended up a lot closer to Remy than when she had started. "Were they that bad?" Concern was evident on her up-turned face.

"No," Remy said. He wished she weren't so beautiful. He wished she wouldn't look at him like that, like he was part rogue, part saint. His throat feeling more parched than ever, he lifted the can and took another long drink. "In fact, most of them were damned nice, but Hildy managed to find fault with them anyway. Too young, too old, too sweet, too matter-of-fact, too cool. You name it, she's complained about it this morning."

"I don't understand." Jill crossed her arms in front of her and resumed her pacing.

"This is a big change for her. She needs time to get used to the idea of having a companion before she tries to hire one."

Jill frowned and sent him a harried glare. "If I wait until the last minute, I may not find someone."

Remy paused. "She's going to be released that soon?"

Jill shrugged. "Carole said the swelling in her ankle has gone down drastically. As soon as the pain goes away enough for Hildy to resume walking on her ankle, she can go home. With her arm in the cast, though, she'll still need help bathing and changing clothes, which is why she needs to have a companion. Carole said she's hoping Hildy might be released from the hospital by the end of next week. That's why I set up interviews for this morning. In fact, I had hoped to be here for them myself, but I got hung up on a business call from New York."

"Problems?"

"The usual. Fortunately, I was able to handle them over the phone." Jill watched as Remy finished his drink and tossed the can into the green recycling bin marked Aluminum. She swept a hand through her cloud of mahogany hair, smoothing the chin-length ends into a bell-shaped curve. She frowned thoughtfully. "I guess I'll have to arrange for another round of interviews for Aunt Hildy, with another list of applicants."

"I wouldn't do that just yet, Jill. Give her another day or two to adjust to the idea."

Jill walked out into the sunlight at the other end of the porch. "And let her think this is going to be a temporary arrangement, just to humor me?" Jill said dryly.

Her words had a familiar ring. "Overheard that, too, hmm?" he quipped.

"Yes, I did, and honestly, Remy, there's no reason for you to be giving my aunt the impression I am worrying about her unnecessarily."

Remy joined Jill at the edge of the hospital sun porch. "I agree, you need to find someone for Hildy," he said gently, meeting her eyes. "But I also think you need to stop pushing Hildy to hire someone right this second. If you give Hildy a chance to adjust to the idea of having live-in help first, chances are she'll be much more amenable to hiring someone."

Jill studied the toe of her high-heeled shoe. "I suppose you're right. I *have* been pushing my aunt." She glanced up, her emotions in tight control. "I'm sorry if I misjudged you earlier."

Remy grinned. "Yeah, well, you shouldn't eavesdrop on other people. It'll trip you up every time."

Jill registered his remark with a wan look but made no comment. With a beleaguered sigh, she glanced at her watch. "We better get back. Hildy is going to wonder what's keeping us."

When they returned to the hospital room, Hildy was sitting in her bed again, reading a magazine. The covers were drawn up to her waist. "There you are!" Hildy smiled at Remy and Jill, picking up the conversation as if the two of them had never been out of the room. "So, darling, did you get your work done last night?"

Jill nodded, looking both happy and relieved. "I faxed the pages to my assistant this morning before coming to the hospital, so I'm all done with my work for the next few days. I hope, anyway," Jill amended with a small sigh. "There's no telling what might come up."

"It hasn't been a problem so far, has it, your staying in Louisiana?" Hildy asked.

Jill's expression was guarded as she replied, "To my surprise, thus far I've been able to handle everything that has come up by either phone or fax." She made no guarantee, however, that the situation would remain that simple to manage, Remy noted. He wondered how people lived with that kind of nonstop pressure on them all the time.

Hildy looked at Remy. "Jill hasn't taken a real vacation in years. Just a day or two off here and there."

Jill blushed. "I've had plenty of long weekends, Aunt Hildy!"

"That's what I mean, sweetheart. Just a day or two off here and there—no real vacations."

Remy looked at Jill. Unable to help himself, he teased, "Too much work and no play makes Jill a dull girl."

Jill rolled her eyes. Remy knew Jill preferred her life this way. That was part of the problem. He wondered if she would feel differently if she realized how exciting everyday life could be, even in rural Louisiana.

They were interrupted by a rap on the hospital door. Carole Destrehan came in, Hildy's chart in hand. "How's my favorite patient?" she asked.

Hildy smiled at her doctor warmly, then complained, "The ankle still hurts."

"Hmm...." Carole walked over to the bed. She set down her chart on the bedside table, drew back the covers and unwrapped the Ace bandage on Hildy's ankle. "It's looking better though, Hildy."

"Yes, it is. In fact, I think it feels well enough to allow me to get out of the hospital, just for a few hours, as long as I stay in my wheelchair. What do you say?"

"What's the big occasion?" Carole asked, rewrapping Hildy's ankle.

"Her garden club is meeting at Magnolia Place on Saturday afternoon," Jill said.

"And I don't want to miss it," Hildy emphasized.

"I could be available to help transport Hildy," Remy offered. "You know, get her in and out of the wheelchair and the car."

Carole looked at all three of them, then turned back to Hildy. "All right, Hildy, you win. You've got a one-day pass, but you have to swear to me you won't overdo it while you're out."

"You have my word as a Southern lady," Hildy promised.

Carole made a note on the chart, then started for the door. She paused next to Remy on the way out. "I'm still waiting for that call," she teased.

Remy caught the miffed look on Jill's face. Was she jealous? Nah. No chance of that. "I haven't forgotten," he drawled. Nor did he have any intention of making that call. Carole Destrehan was a very beautiful woman and capable doctor, but the sparks just weren't there. The kinds of sparks Remy wanted in a relationship with a woman were the kind he seemed to get only with Jill.

"See that you don't," Carole said, then nearly collided with a spry older woman coming in the door. Carole switched her chart to her other hand. "Hello, Maizie."

"Dr. Destrehan." Maizie smiled at Hildy's doctor, then went straight for Hildy, gave her a big hug and a bouquet of pink carnations. While Carole slipped out and Remy cleared a place on the dresser for the carnations, Maizie turned to Jill. "Jill, how wonderful you look!"

Maizie didn't look so bad herself, Remy thought as he put the carnations among the many others that had been delivered to Hildy since her hospitalization.

At age seventy, Maizie was fit and trim. Her blond curls formed a soft fluffy cap around her head and her pale green eyes were vibrant with life. As usual, Maizie was dressed femininely—but practically—in a light blue sweater embroidered with fluffy white clouds, and matching powder blue slacks.

Remy also knew that like Hildy, Maizie had undergone a bad time recently. "How are you, Maizie?" Remy enveloped the petite woman in a hug.

"Oh, about as well as can be expected," Maizie said, a little thickly.

"I was sorry to hear about Murray," Jill said.

"I know you were, and the card and flowers you sent were both lovely." Maizie paused, shook her head, as she perched comfortably on the windowsill opposite Hildy's bed. "You know, after almost a year of being a widow you would think I would be used to living alone by now, but it seems to get harder instead of easier. Maybe it's the fact that we lived in the same house together for near on fifty years, or the fact that we never had any children of our own and all my other family is gone now, but I just can't seem to get used to Murray not being there with me. I keep expecting him to walk in the door or phone or something...." She laughed sadly. "Crazy, isn't it?"

"Perfectly understandable is more like it," Jill said gently. She took a seat on the other side of Maizie and took her wrinkled hand in hers. "I don't know how you'd ever get over a loss like that."

Maizie smiled at Jill. "I guess the answer is you don't. You just go on. But enough maudlin talk." Maizie wiped the moisture from her eyes. "What is this I hear about our garden club meeting on Saturday? I thought it was canceled, but I had a message on my machine that said it was still on, and at your place, Hildy?" she asked in amazement.

"That's right." Hildy grinned triumphantly. "I even got a day pass from Dr. Destrehan to attend."

"Great!" Maizie looked at Remy. "You're going to be there, too, aren't you, Remy darling?"

"I wouldn't miss it for the world," Remy said. Hildy and her friends were a hoot. The older they got, the more mischievously outspoken they were. He enjoyed being around them.

"Remy's going to run the video camera of the botanist's presentation for the club video," Hildy added.

Maizie shook her head and gave Remy an affectionate glance that was not lost on Jill. "Such a sweetheart," Maizie said.

Remy didn't mind running the video camera; he'd done it plenty of times before. He did mind the way Jill was looking at him, as if he were taking blatant advantage of older women. He wished she would begin to trust him. He wanted to get past this sizing-each-other-up stage.

"If Maizie is going to be here for a while—" Jill began.

"Yes, I am, darling," Maizie said.

"Then I'll go on home, I think," Jill said, as she collected her purse and a stack of thank-you notes that needed to be stamped and mailed for Hildy. "I have a lot to do to get ready for the party on Saturday." She walked over to the bed and bent to kiss her aunt goodbye. "You take care of yourself, now, and call me if you need anything at all, Aunt Hildy," Jill said.

"I will, and don't you work too hard," Hildy admonished.

Jill smiled in a way that lit up the entire room. "I won't."

"Remy, darling, if you wouldn't mind..." Hildy said, as Jill exited the room.

Remy smiled at the older woman's obvious matchmaking. "I'll walk Jill down to her car."

Remy caught up with Jill and together they walked to the elevator. Jill didn't look at him. In fact, she seemed a little nervous now that she was alone with him. Not scared nervous, but fidgety nervous. Restless. He knew the feeling well. He felt that way every time he was around her. There was so much he wanted to do and say where she was concerned. But she was sending out a force field of prickliness that was enough to keep the most determined man away. One minute she trusted him, the next she didn't. He sighed, wondering if that would ever change.

"So, what are your plans for the rest of today?" Remy asked. He had already passed on a paying job with another customer to work on the rewiring at Magnolia Place.

"Mostly errands," Jill said. As they stepped out into the sunlight, Remy saw the shadows beneath her eyes that even careful application of makeup couldn't cover.

"Sure you don't just need a nap instead?" he teased lightly, wishing, like Hildy, that Jill would ease up a little and take life at a slower pace.

Jill stiffened and sent him a withering glare.

Too late, Remy realized the innuendo she'd read into the words. He swore silently to himself. Was this woman ever going to give him the benefit of a doubt?

"Thank you ever so much, Remy Beauregard, but I don't need you to tell me when to get in or out of my bed," she said.

Ouch, Remy thought. *She's not just tired, but grouchy, too.* "Sorry," he said.

They passed his pickup truck. "You don't have to escort me all the way to my car," Jill said.

"I know, but I want to," Remy said casually, following her over to the sedan. He paused, not sure why he wanted to delay the moment they parted, but he did.

Jill stared up at him and as Remy stared back, longing went through him, fierce and bittersweet. He felt the way he had when he was a kid, looking in a candy store window, wanting everything, and knowing he had no money to buy anything. Only, he wasn't a kid anymore. And maybe Jill Sutherland wasn't as off-limits as he thought. Maybe she just needed to let her hair down after working so hard on her soap. Tonight was Friday, after all. Everyone deserved a break on the weekend. Maybe if Jill took a break those shadows beneath her eyes would disappear. "Say, how would you like to go to Tippitino's and eat crawfish and work in some dancing later on?" Remy asked impulsively.

For a moment, a very brief moment, he thought Jill looked tempted. But the fun-loving moment faded as soon as it had appeared and she was her old uncompromising self. "I don't have time for dancing," she said tightly. Brushing past him, she worked without much success to get her key in the lock.

Remy took the keys from her and undid the lock himself. "Sure you do, sugar." He removed her keys from the lock and handed them back; their hands brushed lightly, provocatively, in the process. "Everybody has time to go dancing. This is Louisiana, remember?"

Jill regarded him smugly. "Oh, I remember, but I don't have time for dancing, and I would think you wouldn't either, Remy Beauregard," she chastised, waving a finger beneath his nose. "At least not until my aunt's house is completely rewired. Now if you'll be so kind as to excuse me." She tossed her purse onto the car seat and climbed behind the steering wheel with a rustle of silk and pearls. "I've got to find something to fill out those centerpieces for the party tomorrow."

FACE IT, JILL THOUGHT as she meandered among the aisles of the farmers' market scant minutes later, looking for fresh flowers for the centerpieces, *I was rude to Remy. Embarrassingly rude. Why? Because he gets to me. When I think I'm being so clever, he sees right through me. When I think I'm being so cool, he sees right through me.*

She also suspected that Remy knew it wasn't the liquor in Gator's antidote cum aphrodisiac that had gotten to her so much as the sensual magnetism of his presence. Remy Beauregard was everything she had ever warned herself to stay away from: charming, fun-loving, mischievous and completely disarming. He had a way with women and men alike, and a natural zest for life she admired. No matter what happened, he somehow managed to put on a cheerful, easygoing facade. He was also impossibly laid-back; his when-ever-it-gets-done-it-gets-done attitude about the re-wiring of Magnolia Place proved that. And that was something she just couldn't handle. Like oil and water, their personalities just wouldn't mix.

Nevertheless, when she was with Remy, she had the feeling there was nothing the two of them couldn't handle if they just put their minds to it and worked together. That bothered her, too. The more they were together, the more she was attracted to him. Not superficially, but in a heart-pounding, soul-deep way.

Just admit it, she counseled herself sternly. *You want to make love with the man.* Even knowing there was no way the two of them could ever be together in the long run, she wanted to make love with him.

Chapter Eight

The first thing Jill noticed when she returned to Magnolia Place was there was no place to park. The second was that the long winding drive looked like a pickup truck convention. Tucking her car between the mailbox and the last truck, Jill got out and picked up an armload of flowers from the back seat.

No sooner had she stepped onto the front porch than Remy swaggered outside. "Here," he said, taking the bundle of long-stemmed carnations, daisies and greenery from her arms, "let me get those for you."

Jill wished she wasn't so glad to see him. Worse, she still felt bad for snapping at him earlier. "Remy, what's going on here?" she asked as she transferred her handbag to her other hand.

He shrugged, his tool belt jangling around his hips as he led the way inside. "I called a few electrician friends. They're helping to finish the rewiring tonight."

Jill followed him past the workers congregating in the front parlor to the kitchen. She put the flowers in the refrigerator, then straightened to face him. "A few?'' she said, over the whine of a power drill. "It looks—and sounds—more like a dozen.''

"Yep.'' Remy crossed his arms in front of him and gave her a self-satisfied grin. "I'm going to owe them all favors, but it'll be worth it to have the house totally rewired before the party tomorrow. That way,'' he finished gently, "you won't have to worry about it any more or suffer the inconvenience of having me underfoot at all hours of the day and night.''

His words brought back a flurry of memories. Remy, being duped into drinking Kizzie's Love Potion #5 right along with her...Remy, bringing her chicory and coffee and beignets in bed...Remy, rushing over to help her locate the problem when someone had shut off all the power in the house.... Up until now, she had viewed him as nothing more than a pain. Now, confronted with the fact that she might not be seeing him nearly so often in the future, she was forced to realize how much she had counted on his unpredictable presence to liven up her days.

"About what I said when we were leaving the hospital...'' Jill began reluctantly. Now that she saw how far he was going to help her and her aunt out, she wished she had turned down his request for a date with more grace.

Remy cut her off with the judicious lift of his hand. "You were right,'' he said with a chastising frown. "I shouldn't have been thinking about going out dancing tonight when I hadn't finished making good on my promise to your aunt. It was just...you looked so tired. I knew how hard you'd been working, and I thought—wrongly, I know now—that you might want to go out and celebrate the fact you had finished the story line bible for your soap. Believe me, it's not a mistake I'll make again."

Too late, she saw she'd hurt his feelings with her rude behavior. She had to do something to rectify the situation immediately. "Remy—"

"What?"

She bit her lip, trying to figure out how to make it up to him, then asked impulsively, "How long do you think the rewiring is going to take?"

He lifted a broad shoulder in an aimless shrug. "Can't say for sure, but I doubt we'll be done much before midnight."

So much for asking him out to dinner, tonight anyway. A glance at her watch showed it was nearly suppertime now. And now that Jill needed Kizzie around to lend a hand, Kizzie of course was nowhere in sight. "Have you made arrangements to feed these men?" Jill asked.

Remy nodded at the stack of large metal lunch pails in the corner. "Everyone brought their own supper, then they're all going over to my place afterward. I've got some beer on ice over there. I'll probably run into town and get some take-out pizzas or something to go with it, depending on what everyone wants."

Jill looked into her aunt's refrigerator; it was stocked with food, but most of the food was of the feminine variety and slated for the garden club luncheon the next day. Determined nevertheless to repay some of Remy's kindness with some of her own, Jill straightened and asked, "Where's Kizzie?"

"She left when the men showed up. It was clear she wasn't going to get much done with all the men underfoot. She promised to come back tomorrow, first thing, to get ready for the party tomorrow afternoon, so don't you worry about that. Everything'll be just right for the garden club. We won't let your aunt down."

"Thanks. But about the men, Remy... Aunt Hildy would shoot me if she knew they went to all this trouble for us and then we just fed them take-out and beer." Jill did some rapid calculations. "What do you say I go over to your place and take care of the food preparations there?"

Remy looked surprised and pleased all at once. "That'd be great," he said slowly, "but I'm not sure what I have in the refrigerator."

"Don't worry, Remy. I can handle the grocery shopping, too. You just worry about the rewiring. And Remy..." She stood on tiptoe, braced both hands on the width of his strong shoulders and gave him a light kiss on the cheek. "Thanks. I really appreciate this."

"I CAN'T THANK YOU enough for what you did for me and the other men tonight," Remy said as the last guest left.

"Then we're even," Jill smiled back at him warmly, "because I can't thank you enough for seeing that the rewiring was finished." She loaded a tray with empty plates and carried them to his kitchen. She cast a glance over her shoulder. "Did you get enough to eat?"

"I think everyone did," Remy replied. Jill had gone all out, making dozens of hero sandwiches, a huge pot of gumbo, a fruit tray and several rich desserts. He looked at the clock. It was nearly 2:00 a.m. but he wasn't the least bit sleepy and Jill still seemed to be operating on high gear, too. "What about you?" he asked. "Did you get some praline cheesecake?"

Her wistful look faded almost as soon as it appeared. "I usually don't eat such rich desserts."

"But you crave it anyway, don't you?"

She grinned and removed the apron she'd put on over her beige silk pantsuit. "I guess I've earned the calories tonight." She cut herself a small slice while Remy poured them each a fresh cup of coffee. "It's such a pretty night. Let's take our coffee and sit on the glider out back," he said.

"You've talked me into it." Jill waited while he lit the outdoor candles on each side of the glider, then took a seat beside him. They touched from shoulder to knee as they drifted back and forth, but this once, Remy noted, Jill didn't seem to mind his closeness.

"You really love it here, don't you?" Jill said. She took a bite of the cheesecake, and let it melt on her tongue.

Remy nodded. His throat was dry as he watched her savor the rich dessert. He wondered absently if she made love the same way—slowly, and with such finesse. "I guess I'm like your aunt Hildy in that respect. Louisiana is home to me." Deciding it might be okay to get a little more comfortable, he stretched his arm along the back of the glider.

Jill turned toward him, lifting a generous forkful of the creamy dessert to his mouth. Remy took the bite she offered him, and let it rest on his tongue, just as she had.

"Have you ever lived anywhere else?" she asked curiously.

Remy took a sip of his coffee. "California."

Jill turned slightly to the side to put her plate on the patio table next to the glider. "For how long?"

Remy stared at the night sky. A heavy cloud cover obscured all but a few stars. "For a few years after college, while I was working as an electrical engineer."

"But you came back," she guessed.

"Yes," Remy said. "Once this place gets in your blood, you can never get it out."

Jill tipped her face up to his. Her cloud of dark hair was all mussed, her lips bare; she had never looked more beautiful to him than at that moment. "You mean that," she said softly.

Remy nodded. It might sound small town, but the bayous and beaches of Louisiana were home to him, and always would be.

Jill fell silent. They glided back and forth some more. A night breeze blew across their skin. Jill shivered and moved closer into the curve of his arm. Remy wrapped his arm around her shoulders. He liked the way her cheek felt as it rested against his shoulder. He liked the scent of her hair, and the rose of her perfume. It felt right, he decided, being with Jill like this, just as it felt right having her in his home, taking full command of his kitchen.

"You're a true Cajun, aren't you, Remy?" Her voice was soft, almost sleepy with contentment.

Remy tightened the arm he had laced around her shoulders. He continued rocking them back and forth. "Mmm-hmm, and that'll never change. You, on the other hand," he said, tapping her playfully on the nose, "are like Hildy, a Louisiana gentlewoman. Southern, but not really Cajun."

Jill moved out of the curve of his arm and sat up abruptly. "Speaking of being a Southern lady, I really need to go back inside and get those dishes done for you." She vaulted off the glider before he could stop her.

We were getting too close, Remy thought as he watched her go. Her running didn't surprise him. Still, he was disappointed Jill couldn't seem to let herself relax for even a moment. Rising slowly, he followed her inside the small tract home. Jill was at the sink, adding soap and hot water to one side of it. Remy leaned negligently against the kitchen counter. "You don't have to wash the dishes for me, Jill."

The model of efficiency, Jill shook her head. "I couldn't possibly leave you with this mess."

Remy arched a brow. If Jill ran away from him any harder, she'd break both their hearts. "Just like you couldn't possibly allow me to feed the crew I recruited alone?"

Jill rummaged around beneath the sink and came up with an S.O.S. pad clutched firmly in her hand. "As you said, Hildy brought me up right. A true Southern lady never takes advantage or lets a kindness go unrewarded."

Remy's mouth crooked up wryly. He knew what kind of reward he'd like, but he doubted Jill would go for it. Deciding if he couldn't stop her from cleaning up, he might as well join her, he gathered up a handful of dirty dishes and sauntered over to join her at the sink. "It's more than that, isn't it?" Remy guessed, as he dumped them unceremoniously in the soapy water.

Jill frowned and continued to concentrate on her chore. "I admit I don't want to feel like I'm beholden to you...."

Remy grasped her shoulders lightly. He waited for her to look at him. "Just to me, or to anyone?" he asked quietly.

"Anyone," Jill said firmly. She swallowed and stepped back, out of reach. "I like knowing my debts are paid." She turned back to the sink and resumed her dishwashing with a maddening sense of commitment.

"Because your father's weren't?"

Jill slowed slightly, then stopped scrubbing altogether. She held up a casserole for inspection. Finding it clean, she rinsed it and set it in the drainer. "Let me guess. Hildy has been talking again."

Remy picked up a dish towel and began to dry. "She told me your father had a way of charming whatever he needed out of people."

"What a polite way of saying it," Jill murmured.

Remy studied her displeased expression and noted the faint hint of color in her cheeks. "How would you say it?"

Jill's dark blue eyes grew cloudy; she couldn't quite meet his gaze. "My father was a con man. His specialty was charming wealthy women into letting him live off their money."

"You know this for a fact?"

"Until I was about eight, he used me to help him do it."

Remy suffered Jill's hurt right along with her. "And your mother...?" He was unable to imagine being disillusioned at such a young age. No wonder Jill was sometimes cynical to the bone.

"She died when I was two, from complications of pneumonia. Prior to that, according to Hildy, she helped my father set up various get-rich-quick schemes that generated a lot of up-front money but never seemed to pan out in the final analysis. When she died, Dad was left working alone, so he used me to elicit sympathy from unsuspecting women. The fact that he was a single father disarmed many potential 'investors.'

"In fact, it worked great, until I began to realize what was going on. Don't ask me how, but even at a very young age, I knew that what he was doing to people—promising them the moon but delivering nothing—was wrong. So I spoke up. He explained to me very kindly that these women had much more money than they could ever use, and he, having already run through the last of the money he had inherited, was in desperate need of money if he was ever going to be rich again. So I was to keep quiet. Only I couldn't seem to do that."

Remy frowned and continued drying dishes, just as Jill continued washing and rinsing. He knew how close to the surface Jill's emotions ran. He could imagine her ne'er-do-well father's fury when her instinctive sense of right and wrong screwed up his plans. And again, his heart ached for her.

"So how did you end up with Hildy?" he asked as Jill drained the water and began wiping the counters. Finished, she folded the damp dishcloth neatly over the divider between the two stainless-steel sinks.

Arms crossed in front of her, she turned around to face him. She offered him a pragmatic smile. "My father left me with Aunt Hildy and Uncle Augustus when I was eight. It was just supposed to be for a couple of weeks, but as you might imagine, he kept delaying the date of his return, and in the end, he never got around to picking me up. After a year or two, he finally ended up signing some papers making them my legal guardians."

Remy wanted to hug Jill, but her body language was very clear; it said Hands Off. Sensing she needed some space, he backed off slightly. "I'm sorry." The words sounded lame after all she had been through.

Jill shook her head and touched the back of his hand gently, letting him know it was all right, that she didn't know what to say or do in a situation like this, either. "Don't be. Aunt Hildy and Uncle Augustus made me feel very loved and adored when I was growing up. Hildy wasn't able to have children and they had always wanted a family, so it worked out well in the end."

Maybe, Remy thought, but Jill was still carrying some of the hurt around in her heart. No doubt, that was why she mistrusted him so much.

Taking her hand, he led her to one of the stools at the breakfast bar. "Where's your father now?"

Jill sat as Remy refilled their coffee mugs. "He died years ago, in a boating accident in Monte Carlo." Sensing correctly that he was about to offer sympathy again, she held up a hand. He could tell by the look on her face that she was afraid of him getting too close to her. Remy was afraid the next few weeks would pass and he wouldn't get close enough.

Jill released a weary sigh. She took a deep draft of coffee, then set down her cup and traced the rim with her fingertips. "I didn't grieve for him then," she said softly. "And I felt so guilty about it. After all, rogue or not, he was my father. But when I reached down into my heart, there was nothing there."

"Maybe you'd just said your goodbyes years ago, when he left you," Remy supposed gently. He knew in her place he would have.

"Maybe." Jill's lip trembled and, looking more exhausted than ever, she lifted the cup to her lips and took another sip.

She looked so embarrassed and ashamed of all she had told him, not just about herself but about her father, too, that it tore him up inside. Suddenly so much about her—the chip she had on her shoulder, the way she seemed always having to prove herself, to take absolute control of situations and those around her—made sense. She had been coerced into acting less than ethically once; she wasn't going to let it happen to her again. Nor was she willing to let herself be taken advantage of, loved or abandoned. Unfortunately, her efforts to protect herself were perhaps more isolating than she realized.

Acting on instinct, Remy circled around the breakfast bar and wrapped a consoling arm around her slender shoulders. "What your father did happened a long time ago. It doesn't reflect on you, Jill." He certainly didn't think any less of her.

Her lips curled bitterly. Her chin lifted contentiously, in a way that let him know he was stepping on thin ice. Her eyes gleamed wetly, but no tears fell. "More Cajun wisdom, Remy?" she asked in a low, ragged voice.

Remy smiled and sat down on the stool next to hers. The prickly Jill he could handle. He took both her hands in his. "I know you think being Cajun means being charming," he began cautiously.

"And so do you, obviously," she quipped dryly, making no move to extricate her soft warm hands from his sheltering grip.

"But it's more than that. A lot more," Remy said, holding her eyes as he struggled to find a way to explain the principles that guided his life. "It's a way of looking at things...a condition of the heart and mind...of being in a state of euphoria over life as it is today, right now, this moment, without worrying about the past. Cajuns celebrate who they are and who they've become, not who they were, or who their father was, Jill. For a Cajun, the past is irrelevant, just as worrying about the future is a waste of time." Now was all that mattered. The two of them.

"I'm not sure I could ever feel that way." Jill sighed. "As much as I try not to, I agonize over each little mistake. I want so much to be perfect." To have nothing to apologize for.

"You are perfect," he said. Faults and all. He wouldn't trade her for the world.

But again, she discounted his opinion. "No. I'm still trying to prove myself professionally."

Remy thought of all the awards Hildy bragged on about constantly, the hours Jill put in. She had success, all right, but she wasn't nearly as happy as she deserved to be. "There's more to life than being a workaholic and an overachiever, Jill."

Jill lifted her head. Her dark blue eyes sparkled. "Oh yeah, like what?" she sassed.

His heart thudding heavily against his ribs, Remy tugged her off the stool, stood and drew her into his arms. "There's this." He gently brushed the hair from her face, and bent to kiss her with the gentle reverence she deserved. She was soft and malleable in his arms, and far too vulnerable. He could feel the need pouring out of her, the yearning, sweet and fierce. Beneath that lay fear. Jill might have been physically intimate before, but he was willing to bet she had never opened her heart to anyone as much as she had opened her heart and soul to him tonight. As much as he ached to make love to her, here and now, tonight, he couldn't betray that trust. He couldn't take advantage. The time would come, he promised himself, as he slowly ended the sweet lingering kiss. And when it did, there wasn't an inch of her he wouldn't know.

She was trembling when he let her go.

He was just as shaken. "I better get you home," Remy said gruffly. He didn't want to leave her, but he knew he must. Otherwise, there was no telling what might happen between them.

Looking just as reluctant to part company as he was, Jill tucked her hair behind her ear. While he watched, she carried her cup to the sink and rinsed it carefully. Her expression neutral, she turned back around to face him. "Before I go, I need something from you," she said.

I need something from you, too, Remy thought wistfully. Another kiss, and then another... but that wasn't going to happen, not tonight. Not until the time was one hundred percent right. He met her eyes. "Name it."

"Do you have the names and addresses of the men who helped you do the rewiring?"

Remy had braced himself for just about anything, except that request. He frowned, thinking again about how late it was and how tired she looked. "They're in my Rolodex, on the desk in the den. What are you going to do?"

"Copy them down so Hildy and I can send them thank-you notes, and maybe some baskets of fresh fruit."

Of course, Remy thought. Jill wouldn't want to owe anyone anything. And that probably included him. He wondered if he would get a fruit basket, too. He would be irked to be lumped in with all the other guys, as far as she was concerned.

"Would you mind if I copied them down before I go home?" Jill asked. "That way I can take care of my thank-yous first thing in the morning."

"No problem. While you're doing that, I'll take the trash out and dump the ice out of the washtubs."

It took about fifteen minutes for Remy to sort the recyclables in the appropriate bins, dry and put away the washtubs in the garage. Finished, he went into the kitchen to wash his hands, and then into the den to see if Jill was ready to go home.

He paused in the doorway of the den, smiling at what he saw. Jill was curled up in a corner of the sofa, the list of names on her lap, her head resting on her arms. She was sound asleep.

Belatedly, Remy remembered what Jill had said to her aunt about being up most of the previous night, working to finish her soap's story bible for next year. She'd spent the rest of the day running around getting things for the garden club centerpieces. Then shopped and cooked for a crowd that night. No wonder she was dead on her feet! The only real surprise, in Remy's estimation, was that she'd lasted this long.

Deciding the sooner they got her home the better, he walked over to touch her arm gently. "Jill?"

She slept on. He touched her again. "Jill, sugar, time to wake up and go home."

Again, she barely stirred.

Realizing how utterly exhausted she was, Remy decided it would be cruel to wake her. The best thing would be to carry her to his bed, and let her spend the night there. Morning would come soon enough, and with it the preparations for the garden club meeting at Magnolia Place.

He slid a hand beneath her hips and another around her shoulders. He lifted her against his chest. As he strode to the bedroom and lowered her gently to the bed, she stirred softly in her sleep and her hands curled around the fabric of his shirt. Remy tried to extricate her fingers. She let go and grabbed him around the middle, hugging him to her like a pillow. Her actions had him so off-balance, it was either lower himself to the bed or fall down. He lowered himself to the bed. Still using his chest as a pillow for her head, she cuddled closer. Remy groaned and fell back against the pillows. If she woke now, she was really going to be ticked off at him.

Fortunately, he reassured himself, she was so sound asleep, she was *not* going to wake. All he had to do was lie here for a few minutes, until he could extricate himself from her slumberous embrace, and then he'd head for the sofa.

In the meantime, he couldn't say he really minded holding her in his arms all that much. Jill was a remarkably cuddly woman when she wasn't so busy fighting her feelings for him. Her fluffy mahogany hair was soft and thick, her silky skin scented faintly with roses and the sweet essence that was Jill.

It would be so easy to fall in love with her, he thought, potion or no potion. She might see herself as an all-driven career woman, but there was a softer side to Jill, too. She had a boundless capacity for love, shown by the depth of feelings she had for her aunt. She was smart and sassy and funny. She'd make a wonderful wife and mother, but chances were she'd never slow down long enough to get married again and become a mother...unless something happened to make her see that she was wrong to categorically rule out marriage, just because Jake, like her father, had walked out on her as soon as the going got tough.

Chapter Nine

Jill woke to the fragrant scent of Remy's cologne. She was surrounded by warmth, cuddled against a solid male chest, with a long sexy male leg inserted between the two of hers.... Her eyes flew open. "Oh, God!" She sat up suddenly, her heart pounding. Her throat was dry.

Remy's eyes opened slowly. He was lying on his back beside her. He looked just as disoriented, though a heck of a lot happier than she felt. Where the hell were they? Jill wondered. How had they gotten here? "Whose bed is this?" Jill demanded.

"Mine." Remy shoved the sandy brown hair from his eyes and struggled to sit up.

Jill ran her tongue across her lips. Damn, but she was thirsty. Hungry, too. And no wonder. She'd had very little to eat or drink yesterday. "How did I get here?"

"I carried you here last night after you fell asleep. Don't you remember?"

She shot him an irritated glance. "No! I don't remember that!" she denied hotly. "Not at all!" Though, now that she thought about it, Jill did have a rather fuzzy memory of being held against Remy's chest…being carried…cuddling against him…. He'd been so warm and strong and solid, exactly what she needed.

Oh, no! Wondering what else might have happened, she glanced down at herself in a panic. Thank God her buttons were all done, her clothing—except for her shoes—on. Remy, however, was not so thoroughly dressed. His shirt was unbuttoned and open to the waist, the top button of his fly undone.

He caught her assessing glance. "Hey." Remy sat up and raised both hands in surrender. "Nothing happened."

Jill put a trembling hand to her aching head. She wasn't hung over from alcohol, but she felt hung over with accumulated fatigue. She massaged her aching temples with her fingers. "It seems to me I remember a kiss," she said in a voice that shook.

"A sweet one, in the kitchen before you fell asleep, nothing more."

"Then how did I get here?" she cried. Scrambling to the edge of the bed, she looked around for her shoes.

Remy caught her by the waist and dragged her back to sit beside him. "I was going to take you home, but you wanted to copy those names and addresses from the Rolodex. While you were busy with that, I took the trash out to the recycling bins in the garage. I was gone about fifteen minutes. When I came back inside, I found you curled up on the sofa, fast asleep. I tried to wake you several times, but you were out like a light."

Jill had a dim memory of Remy touching her shoulder and murmuring something annoying in her ear. Obviously, he hadn't tried very hard to wake her. She was a very light sleeper. "So you just went to bed with me? Is that it?" she cried, incensed.

"No, of course not." He snapped his jeans and buttoned his shirt with quick efficient movements. "I carried you in here. I put you down, but you got ahold of my shirt. I tried to pry your hands loose. I'd almost succeeded when you bear hugged me around the middle and used my chest as a pillow. So I just lay down beside you. I didn't intend to fall asleep myself, but I was pretty damn tired, too."

That apparently was the end of the story. "Oh, God, I can't believe this." Jill vaulted off the bed and hobbled toward the living room. She was stiff and sore all over from sleeping in one position all night.

Remy trailed after her. "C'mon, Jill. I know you were married. It's not as if you've never slept with a man before!"

Jill found her shoes between the coffee table and the sofa. She put a hand on the back of the sofa to steady herself and slipped them on. "We didn't sleep together! Not the way you mean."

Remy clamped his hands on his hips and regarded her exasperatedly. "I meant . . . sleep. Not make love. And that's exactly what we did last night, Jill, sleep together, not make love. What's the big deal?"

The big deal was that sleeping with him was in many ways just as intimate as making love would have been. The big deal was she had woken, to find herself in his arms. And, before she had realized the implications, she had actually liked it.

"Remy, please." Jill found her list of names. She stuffed it into her purse and removed her hairbrush. She tugged it through her hair, unable to recall when she had ever felt so self-conscious.

Remy tucked his shirttail into his jeans. The look he gave her was conciliatory. "This wasn't such a big deal, Jill."

Maybe not for him, Jill thought, but for her it was. She had awakened, feeling like she was in sweet heaven, only to find out she was one giant step closer to sleeping with Remy Beauregard. Well, he had another think coming if he thought she was going to get involved with him. She'd already had too many regrets in her life. She wasn't cut out for one-night stands or brief affairs. She wasn't capable of separating the physical from the emotional when it came to loving a man. If she made love with a man, she did it heart and soul. There was no future for her and Remy. Her life was in New York. His was here. Last night he had said this place was in his blood . . . he had lived elsewhere and come back. He never intended to leave again.

Therefore, no matter how tempting it seemed, no matter how much a part of her longed to see where this passion simmering between them would lead, she was not going to get involved with Remy Beauregard.

The phone rang and Remy walked over to get it. "Hello. Hi, Hildy. Yeah, she's here." He sent Jill a helpless look. "She, uh . . . she wanted to discuss the garden club meeting this afternoon, to know if I had a video camera or if she needed to rent one. I told her I had one, but I need to buy some film for it.'' He paused, listening hard, his eyes still on Jill. "Sure, I can be at the hospital to get you in about an hour, Hildy, just as soon as I've had a shower...."

Jill didn't want to hear anymore. She rushed out the door and drove home in record time. She walked in the front door, feeling disheveled and out of sorts, only to come face-to-face with Kizzie, who was dressed in the usual housedress and combat boots and had a stack of starched linen tablecloths in her arms. Her eyes widened speculatively as she looked over Jill.

Jill was not about to discuss where she'd spent the night with the person who had started this mess in the first place, with her folksy love potion.

Acting as if it were perfectly normal for her to be wearing the same clothes she'd had on the previous day and looking as if she had just tumbled out of bed, Jill marched past Kizzie and into the kitchen. She half expected it to be strung with clotheslines and sheets, since it was like Kizzie to make things as difficult as possible. Instead, the kitchen was neat and orderly. Pecan pies sat cooling on the counter. The makings for stuffed mushrooms and puff-pastry cheese straws were on the counter. Rich gumbo simmered on the stove. An amazing variety of small tea sandwiches and a beautiful fruit salad were already prepared and in the refrigerator.

Jill turned to Kizzie in amazement. "I can't believe how much you've done already," she said, stunned. Kizzie had followed Jill's instructions to the letter.

"It was no problem," Kizzie said nonchalantly. "I also brought the folding tables down from the attic and set them out back on the veranda. I assume you'll be wanting to make the centerpieces up yourself?"

Still feeling a little stunned, Jill murmured, "Yes, I do. Thank you, Kizzie. I'll get started on the centerpieces right away, just as soon as I've had a shower."

"Will you be wanting some breakfast, or did you already have breakfast wherever it was that you spent the night last night?" Kizzie asked slyly. "Perhaps at that Remy Beauregard's house...?"

Jill stiffened. Here we go again, Jill thought. Obviously, Kizzie had seen Jill's car parked in front of Remy's house, probably on her way to work. Jill gave Kizzie the smile she reserved for the most difficult writers on her staff. "Where I spent the night, Kizzie, is no one's business but my own."

Kizzie gave Jill a skeptical look. "I'm not so sure Miz Hildy would feel that way."

Jill's temper flared. She pointed a warning finger at Kizzie. "Not one word about this to my aunt, Kizzie! And I mean it!" She did not want Hildy or any of Hildy's friends from the garden club speculating on Jill's love life, or lack thereof, with Remy Beauregard.

Kizzie merely grinned and pointed in the direction of Jill's room upstairs. "Your aunt called this morning. She said you'd be wearing your best party dress this afternoon. It's pressed and ready for you."

"WHY, JILL, DARLING, you look lovely today," Aunt Hildy said as Remy wheeled her into the house.

Remy looked at Jill and barely squashed a grin of distinctly male appreciation.

Jill had an idea what he was thinking. The party dress Aunt Hildy had selected for Jill was one she had worn to sorority teas during her college days at Tulane. It was an off-the-shoulder peach chiffon sundress, with a full ruffled skirt. She had pumps that were dyed to match.

"Thank you, Aunt Hildy," Jill said, wishing she didn't feel like such an anachronism. "Your dress is lovely, too." Hildy was wearing a short-sleeved sage green silk dress with a matching shawl, and dyed-to-match ballerina slippers that would accommodate her healing ankle.

"How are the centerpieces coming?"

Jill smiled. She had filled antique copper teakettles with fresh flowers and greenery, and decorated them with velvet ribbons. They were perfect. "They're all set."

Kizzie appeared in the doorway.

To Jill's amazement, Kizzie had changed into a gray linen dress with a white apron, white stockings and tennis shoes. She came forward to greet Hildy. "Nice to have you back, Miz Hildy," she said, almost shyly.

"Nice to be back, Kizzie, even on a day pass!" Hildy grasped Kizzie's hand. "How about wheeling me out to the veranda, Kizzie, so we can look things over and see what still needs to be done?"

"Right away," Kizzie said, so demurely that Jill felt her mouth drop open sightly.

Before she knew it, she and Remy were left alone. He, too, was all dressed up, in a navy blazer, khaki slacks, light blue shirt and tie. His sandy hair was brushed neatly to one side. His dark brown eyes were dancing with mischief. "Well, don't you look like a ripe Georgia peach that just fell off the tree," he drawled.

"Hardy-har-har, aren't you the funny one." Jill crossed her arms in front of her and glared at him. For the thousandth time, she wished she weren't so darn aware of him, and vice versa.

"Still mad at me for last night, huh?" he prodded mischievously.

Jill felt her cheeks heat up. She sent him a warning look. "Don't start." The sound of a car door sent Jill to the window.

"First guest?" Remy said, following Jill to the door.

"Elanore. I haven't seen her in ages." Jill went outside to give one of her former schoolteachers a hug.

"You look good," Elanore, a tall spare woman with gray hair, said.

Jill leaned close enough to whisper. "As you can probably guess, Aunt Hildy chose my dress."

Elanore's eyes sparkled. At sixty-two, she was the youngest member of the garden club. "Somehow I figured that," she said, "but you look lovely anyway. Remy, nice to see you," she added as she made her way briskly up the steps.

Remy stepped forward to help Elanore with the plate of home-baked scones she carried.

"You two know each other?" Jill asked.

"Elanore is a frequent guest at Hildy's Sunday dinners, too," Remy said.

"Although I don't know how much longer that will continue." Elanore paused at the top of the steps. She looked at Jill and Remy both. "Did Hildy tell you the new highway is going right through the center of my home?" Elanore asked indignantly.

Jill and Remy looked at Elanore in mutual sympathy. "Can you move the house?" Remy asked.

Elanore shook her head. "It's too old, the process too expensive. No, sad to say, the house is going to bite the dust, along with all the wonderful memories in it, but those are the breaks."

"I'm sorry," Jill said.

"Thank you, honey."

"What are you going to do?" Remy held the screen door for the women.

"I don't rightly know yet," Elanore confessed as the three of them walked toward the kitchen. Remy set the plate of perfect golden scones on the counter. "My children want me to move in with them, and although I love them dearly, I do not want to do that. The idea of that new retirement home apartment complex in Baton Rouge doesn't appeal, either. But let's not spoil the party with talk about my problems. I'll figure out something," Elanore finished just as Kizzie wheeled Hildy back into the kitchen.

By the time another round of greetings ensued, the second car had arrived, and then the third. Half an hour later, the back porch was full of happy, gossiping women. Remy busied himself setting up the video camera for the presentation later on. Kizzie was filling tall crystal glasses with ice tea.

Jill was a little irritated to see how conventionally Kizzie could dress and behave when she wanted to. She had a feeling that the housekeeper had been doing a number on her, just for spite. "You're a lot more normal than you pretend, aren't you, Kizzie?" Jill said, as she put a sprig of mint in every glass.

Kizzie looked up from the lemon she was slicing. Suddenly, she was ready for battle again with Jill. Jill could just see her dragging out the sheets and the clotheslines. . . .

Remy's shadow fell over them as he walked in the door. "Jill? Hate to interrupt when the two of you are getting on so famously, but may I see you for a moment?"

Jill cast an aggravated look at Kizzie, then another at Remy. She didn't want to go off with him but she didn't want any more scenes with Kizzie, either. "Certainly." Jill followed Remy into the front hall. As they passed the stairs, he grabbed her wrist. The next thing she knew, he was opening the closet door, pulling the light chain, and pushing her inside. She barely had time to draw a breath before he followed, shutting the door behind him.

"Remy, for heaven's sake!" Jill exclaimed furiously. "What are those ladies going to think if they see us in here together?"

"Then you better pipe down, hadn't you, sugar?"

Jill was still extremely embarrassed about having spent the night sleeping in his arms. She folded her arms in front of her and tipped her chin up defiantly. "I was just getting somewhere with Kizzie."

He arched a disapproving sandy brow. "Making things worse is more like it."

The hot, ardent look in his dark brown eyes, coupled with his crazy idea that he suddenly knew what was best for all of them, was very unsettling. "What's that supposed to mean?" Jill demanded stubbornly.

He leaned forward and took her by both arms. He seemed as annoyed by her take-charge attitude as she was by his. "Don't you get it? Kizzie isn't any more comfortable in that maid's outfit she's wearing today than you are in that frilly debutante party dress you've got on. She's just wearing it to please your aunt, same as you are. As soon as those ladies are out of here, Kizzie will be back to normal like a shot."

Jill tensed. "'Normal,' meaning faded housedresses and black combat boots," she guessed.

"You got it."

The small closet gave them very little room to maneuver. Jill leaned back against the coats, hoping Remy would take the hint and let go of her; he didn't. Ignoring the butterflies jumping around in her stomach, she drawled, "Let me get this straight, Einstein. You don't think Kizzie is giving me a hard time on purpose?"

"Oh, she's giving you a hard time, all right, but only because she knows you want to take your aunt back to New York with you."

Jill blew out an exasperated breath. "Aunt Hildy refused to go to New York with me!"

"So?" Remy used his grip on her shoulders to drag her nearer. "Aunt Hildy wants to please you, just like you want to please her. Kizzie knows if you keep pushing your aunt, you'll eventually get your way.''

Jill was silent. His words had the ring of truth. She had seen the affection between Kizzie and her aunt. Before, prior to Hildy's fall, on the weekends and holidays Jill was back in Louisiana, Kizzie hadn't been around as often. ''You make it sound as if I'm just thinking of myself,'' Jill said. She already knew Kizzie felt that way!

''No. I know you have a career there, responsibilities.''

''I have responsibilities here, too, Remy, responsibilities that are just as, if not more, important to me.''

''I know that, too, and I'm trying to tell you that you don't have to worry. I'll take care of your aunt, Jill.''

''You're not family, Remy.''

There was a long pause. His eyes darkened as he silently challenged her. ''Hildy won't hold that against me,'' he said gruffly.

''Maybe not, but—''

Footsteps sounded just outside the closet door. Jill made a face at Remy and silently mouthed a very unladylike word that summed up what she thought of the place he had chosen for their tête-à-tête.

''Jill! Remy darling!'' Elanore called.

''Where are you, darlings?'' Maizie added.

''They must be around here somewhere,'' Frieda said.

''Oh, fiddlesticks,'' Jill whispered. She glared at Remy pointedly and mouthed, ''Now what?'' If word of this got back to the entire garden club, she'd absolutely die.

Remy caught her against him and pressed a single finger to her lips. "Shh," he whispered, his warm breath brushing her ear. Footsteps moved back and forth outside the closet. Jill held her breath and prayed no one noticed the light spilling out from beneath the door.

"I'll check upstairs," Elanore said.

"I'll look in the kitchen," Maizie added.

"I'll stay here in case they come by, on the way to the back porch," Frieda volunteered.

Her heart pounding, Jill stayed pressed against Remy. The smell of cedar in the closet was strong. But the scent of Remy's cologne, so reminiscent of a pine forest on a hot summer's day, was stronger. Jill felt the quiet strength in the arm around her, the muscled surface of his chest. The next thing she knew he was shifting slightly. Still holding her close with one hand, he lifted the other to the back of her neck. Tilting her head back, he looked down into her eyes, and slowly, slowly lowered his mouth to hers.

"Don't," Jill said, but she didn't really mean it and he knew it as he languidly kissed her into submission, kissed her until her knees went weak and she was holding on to him because he was the only stable element in a wildly spinning world.

When at long last he drew away, there was no sound outside the closet door. Only laughter, in the distance, from the back porch.

Inside the closet was another matter. Their breaths were ragged, their hearts pounding, their limbs trembling. He wanted her. Oh, how he wanted her. She saw it in his eyes, and felt it in the rigidness of his body. And she wanted him, too, with an urgency that was fast growing out of control.

Remy rubbed a thumb across Jill's lips, wiping away the dewy residue of their kiss. She shivered in a way that had nothing to do with being cold and everything to do with the feelings between them. Feelings, she was beginning to see, that were going to have to be resolved before she left Louisiana.

Jill sighed. She knew how she wanted these feelings to be resolved, even if it didn't make any sense.

Remy released her reluctantly. "Sounds like the coast is clear," he whispered.

Jill stared up at him and wondered if maybe it was time to start living her life, Cajun-style, one pleasurable moment at a time. The only thing she knew for sure was that her heart was still pounding foolishly, her knees shaking, her insides melting from his kiss.

Unfortunately, this was no time for her to be so wildly excited. "I am going to kill you for this," Jill whispered as she struggled to get her soaring emotions under control. She couldn't believe he'd seduced her into necking in the downstairs hall closet while a garden club meeting was taking place on the back porch. He had to know they were courting absolute disaster here if anyone found out!

Remy merely grinned one of his Cajun bad-boy grins, then opened the door a crack and peered out into the front hall. "Yep, the coast is clear, all right." He switched off the closet light with one hand, then led the way out of the closet. He shut the door quietly after them, then pointed to the porch. "We better join the guests."

"Where are we going to say we've been?" Jill said as she smoothed her hair and headed for the white veranda at the rear of the antebellum home.

Remy shrugged and tucked an errant strand of her hair behind her ear. "We'll just say we were outside, talking privately."

"But—" Jill protested. Surely he realized they needed a better story than that. She started to delay him. Too late, Elanore had seen them.

"Remy! Jill! Come on out here and join us! We've already started on the first course!"

Jill stepped out onto the porch with Remy at her side. Despite her efforts to appear cool and collected, she could feel the heat gathering in her cheeks.

"Where were you, darlings?" Aunt Hildy asked.

Kizzie stepped out behind the two of them, a silver serving platter of cucumber-and-cream-cheese sandwiches in her hands. Jill sent Kizzie a warning look.

Kizzie ignored it cavalierly.

"I know where they were," Kizzie announced, as a breathless hush fell over the ladies assembled on the porch.

Kizzie turned back to Jill with a mischievous grin. "Jill was in the front hall closet with Remy Beauregard. And if you ask me, they were in there for an awfully long time!"

Chapter Ten

Jill turned beet red as feminine gasps were heard all around. Remy, on the other hand, played the part of the charming Cajun rogue for all it was worth. "What can I say, ladies? Hildy's lovely niece has totally bewitched me!"

Giggles followed. "We heard the two of you took Kizzie's famous Love Potion #5!" Maizie said.

"Not to worry," Remy said as he laced an arm about Jill's shoulder. "We stopped by Madame Rousseau's on the way back from New Orleans the other day and took an antidote."

"Doesn't look to me like the antidote worked, judging by the way Jill is still blushing," Elanore said.

"Remy looks a little smitten, too," Frieda remarked.

"I know exactly what you all mean," Aunt Hildy agreed.

Jill stepped out of the warm circle of Remy's arm, determined to put an end to this nonsense here and now. What she'd felt just now in the closet, and last night in the kitchen, and this morning in Remy's bed, were all mere aberrations, the result of being too long between kisses, period. "I assure you, ladies, the antidote worked every bit as well as the potion did."

"And we'll prove it," Remy said, then bent Jill backward from the waist. He delivered a long, soul-searing kiss that Jill felt all the way to her toes. She clung to his shoulders, drowning in the sensations that flowed through her. The breath left her lungs as he continued to kiss her with tender urgency. With a soft, low moan of appreciation, Jill realized he was kissing her like a man who wanted a lifetime commitment from her, not just a moment of pleasure. Giddiness swept through her, more intoxicating than any love potion. Suddenly the future loomed ahead of them like a bright shiny gift.

Only the sound of giggling around them brought her out of it. Abruptly remembering they had an audience hanging on their every word, look and romantic action, Jill put a hand on Remy's chest and pushed. It took a moment, but finally he got the hint. Slowly he lifted his mouth from hers, but to her chagrin he made no immediate move to release her. "I think we've provided enough entertainment for one afternoon, don't you, Remy?" she said.

Remy reluctantly brought Jill all the way back up and released her. He turned to the circles of ladies. "Actually," he said with a wink, "if it were up to me, I could go on kissing this lovely lady forever!"

His mischievous words were followed by another round of gasps and chuckles.

Jill gave Remy a quelling look.

The ladies laughed all the more. "If that's the result, I want some of Kizzie's famous potion!" Frieda said.

Hildy looked at Kizzie. "I think if you were to market your potion, dear, you could make a mint."

Remy looked at Jill with another lazy smile. Fortunately, the arrival of the day's guest speaker, the botanist, saved the day.

"I THINK THE PARTY was a smashing success," Hildy said as Remy and Jill wheeled her back into the hospital.

"I think so, too, Aunt Hildy." Jill moved ahead to press the Up elevator button, then held the door for both of them.

"The botanist's presentation was interesting, too," Remy said, as the doors closed and the elevator shot skyward.

"Wasn't he a treasure!" Hildy said, her eyes sparkling. "We'll have to ask him back!"

The elevator doors opened on Hildy's floor. Again, Jill held the door while Remy steered her aunt's wheelchair out of the elevator. Jill was struck by how good and right it felt to have Remy there with her aunt and herself. It was as if he were family, too. As if he had always belonged there. Unfortunately, Jill's feelings were anything but sisterly toward Remy.

"Good to have you back, Hildy," one of the nurses said as they passed the nurses' station.

"I'm happy to see you, too, but I'd rather be home!" Hildy joked back. They all laughed.

"I'll be in to help you get ready for bed in a moment," the nurse said.

"No rush," Hildy said. The nurse nodded, understanding they wanted a moment alone.

Remy steered the wheelchair into Hildy's private room. After Jill lowered the hospital bed, Remy carefully assisted Hildy from the wheelchair. "You must be awfully tired," he said as Jill drew the covers to her aunt's waist and adjusted the pillows behind her.

"I am, but there's something I want to say to the two of you first," Hildy said, once she was comfortably situated and Remy and Jill were seated on either side of her.

Jill sensed by the expression on her aunt's face their talk was going to be a serious one. She took Hildy's hand in both of hers.

Hildy smiled at her gently. "I know I've been feeling very sorry for myself because I'm beginning to get to the age where it's dangerous for me to live alone. But I realized something today, Jill."

"What, Aunt Hildy?"

"That my circumstances aren't as dreadful as I thought. I'm not the only one facing a life-style change. Maizie, Elanore and Frieda are all looking at similar changes in their lives, so..." Hildy frowned and took a deep breath. "If you really want me to go back to New York with you when you go, Jill, then I'll go. But you don't have to buy a house in Connecticut. Your apartment in Manhattan will do just fine. But—and this is where I will put my foot down—I still don't want a stranger living with us twenty-four hours a day."

"All right," Jill said. Maybe she could just get a nurse companion to come in during the day. Someone nice and friendly to keep her aunt company while Jill was at the studio.

"You're agreeing, just like that?" Hildy asked, amazed. Remy looked similarly shocked.

Jill nodded, afraid deep down that it wasn't going to be as simple as she hoped it would be. "I understand you want your privacy, Aunt Hildy, and I promise you that we'll work something out that pleases both of us," Jill said.

The nurse appeared in the doorway. "Okay, visitors. Out. Hildy needs her rest."

Hildy rolled her eyes, then grinned at Jill and Remy. "You heard the general. I'll see you tomorrow?"

"Of course," Remy and Jill said in unison. They bent to kiss her goodbye, then they left. They were silent until they reached Remy's car, a plushly equipped dark green Ford Taurus. He didn't drive it often. Most of the time he tooled around in his beat-up Beauregard Electric pickup truck. But he had driven the Taurus that day to take Hildy back and forth to the hospital.

He held the door for her, then circled around the front and climbed in behind the wheel. "Everything okay?" He put the key in the ignition, but made no move to start the car. "You look . . . upset."

"I am."

His sandy brow furrowed. "How come? I would think you'd be happy, since you just got everything you wanted, Hildy's agreed to go back to New York with you."

Jill thought of her aunt's excitement about the garden club meeting and how much she loved being with all her friends. She shook her head. "That's not what I want anymore."

Remy took her hand in his and twined their fingers together. "How come?"

Jill lifted her head and met his searching gaze. "Because when I saw her with her friends this afternoon, I saw how happy she was. And I knew that even if I moved to Connecticut in a house with a garden, and found another garden club for Aunt Hildy to join, it wouldn't be the same."

"I know what you mean," Remy interjected gravely. "The growing season in Connecticut is a lot shorter."

Jill punched him playfully in the arm. "I mean, Remy, that new friends are nice, but it's not the same as being with old friends. Elanore, Frieda and Maizie have been through so much with my aunt. They've been friends for over thirty years. Next to me, they're the closest thing to family she has."

"And they're all aging," Remy said.

"Yes. And all facing the same types of situations, just as Aunt Hildy said. And that got me to thinking." Jill turned to Remy excitedly. "What if none of them had to leave the area? What if they could all move in with Hildy? I mean, there's plenty of space. Magnolia Place has twelve rooms, including six bedrooms and six private baths. Maizie is seventy, but Elanore is only sixty-two, Frieda sixty-three. They've got a lot of good years left in them. And with Kizzie around to help with the housework, and you next door to be their Sir Galahad..." Jill tunneled her fingers through her hair, pushing it off her face. She looked to Remy for approval. "Am I crazy to think this could actually work?"

"You're not crazy." Remy took her into his arms and gathered her close. "I think you're the sweetest, kindest, gentlest woman I've ever met." He gently traced the profile of her face with the back of his hand. "Even though you'd just about die before you let me know it." Bending his head, he kissed her gently, then with growing passion. This once, Jill didn't try to fight her feelings. Her time with Remy was dwindling fast. Suddenly she didn't want to waste it. Maybe they didn't have forever. Maybe it had all started with Kizzie's love potion, but that didn't mean they couldn't enjoy it while it lasted...and just for a little while, anyway, take it one day at a time.

The sound of footsteps and a car door slamming made them both acutely aware of their surroundings. Remy moved back slightly. His mouth curved wryly as he studied her. "You realize we've just been necking in a hospital parking lot?"

"I knew you were trouble the first moment I laid eyes on you," Jill teased.

Remy just smiled and continued to look at her. "So, when are you going to tell your aunt about your idea?" he asked.

"As soon as I've talked to Elanore, Maizie and Frieda. I don't want to get Hildy's hopes up, only to crush them again."

"Good thinking. Now, about that love potion..."

Jill groaned. "Remy, please..."

"I mean it, Jill. This kissing in closets and on back porches and in parked cars is most definitely not the behavior of a proper Southern lady." He shook his head in mock chastisement. "I'd be remiss in my duties as a Southern gentleman if I let you continue on indefinitely under the influence of Kizzie's love potion and Gator's aphrodisiac, without at least trying to do something about it first."

Jill's heart pounded as she thought about what that "something" might be.

"And we certainly can't let you go back to New York until we have somehow negated those highly charged chemicals floating around in your bloodstream," Remy continued with mock solemnity.

"Ah, I see. You wouldn't want me to run into someone without your scruples, would you?" Because then, assuming these potions really worked, she might make love with that someone instead of him.

"Absolutely not," he agreed, dark eyes sparkling determinedly.

Jill took a closer look. Beneath the teasing grin, he actually seemed a little jealous and worried about the prospect of losing her to someone else. But maybe that wasn't so unusual given all they had been through together in the past week. She also recalled she felt much the same way when she saw him with the husband-hunting Dr. Carole Destrehan or pictured him with someone—anyone—else.

"You actually think the potion-aphrodisiac mix is that powerful?" Jill asked.

"If you consider the way I've been feeling the past few days, absolutely." He leaned toward her conspiratorially, a teasing grin on his handsome face. "You may not believe it, but I'm not generally prone to necking in cars and closets and back porches myself."

Jill wanted to believe that.

"Which is why," Remy explained logically, "we can't let you go back to New York until we've managed to do something to counter those feelings."

The truth was, the highly romantic, impractical side of Jill was beginning not to want to return to New York at all. And that was crazy. She had a life there, a career she loved, a home, friends. She would be nuts to give up everything she had spent the past nine years building. But that was her first, and at the moment, most powerful inclination. "So what do you suggest?" she asked. She was hoping he'd ask her home with him. She was hoping he'd ask her to make love with him ... if for no other reason than to get him out of her system, and her out of his.   Remy frowned thoughtfully and linked hands with her once again. "Well, you know what we were saying the other day about our reaction to Kizzie's love potion and Gator's aphrodisiac possibly being linked to a very deep level of our subconscious, the primal superstitions that we all have?"

Jill regarded Remy warily. She didn't like the sound of this, even though she was the one who had come up with the theory. "I remember," she said cautiously. But she had said those things when she had desperately wanted to get rid of these feelings she was having for him. Now she wasn't so sure she did. Now she was beginning to want to hang on to them. And she had thought—hoped—Remy was feeling the same.

Had she read more into his tender, playful kisses than there actually was?

"Well, maybe that's why none of the antidotes we've taken so far have worked," Remy proposed theoretically, his expression impassive.

Jill lifted a brow, aware her heart was thudding against her ribs. "Because they weren't from the same person who gave us the potion?"

"No." Remy fitted his hand more intimately against hers. "Because we were skeptical all along that the various antidotes would work when we took the potions."

"Therefore, our subconsciouses wouldn't let the antidotes work," Jill speculated playfully as warmth radiated from her palm, up her arm, into her chest.

"Right." Remy nodded as he slipped his other hand beneath hers, so her palm was cradled on all sides by imposing male heat. He looked into her eyes. "But just suppose for a moment that our subconsciouses really believed that a particular antidote would work?"

Jill began to see where he was going with this. "Then it would probably be successful." The only sound in the interior of the car was the soft metered rhythm of their breaths. "But where would we get such an antidote?" she asked as she groped for reasons why not to give in to the desire plaguing her and kiss him again. She licked suddenly dry lips. "We've already looked high and low and I really *don't* want to drink any more noxious liquids with unknown ingredients."

"Neither do I." Remy shared her sentiments completely. "Which got me to thinking. What if we knew exactly what was in the potions beforehand?"

Jill shrugged. "That'd be great, I guess, but how—"

He held up a palm to stifle her confused flow of words. "When you want to be absolutely certain something is done and done right, what do you do, Jill?"

"You do it yourself." Recognition dawned as she felt, more than ever, that they were beginning to be a team. "You're suggesting we make an antidote ourselves?" What a brilliant idea, and a marvelous excuse to be together.

"I am." He leaned closer, waiting to see her reaction.

His lips were very close to hers. She found she was thinking about kissing him again.

"So what do you think?" he said.

"I think it's a great idea," Jill said. "There's only one problem. Neither of us knows anything about making love potions."

"Yeah, I know. That's why I stopped by the bookstore and the library in Baton Rouge before I picked Hildy up at the hospital this morning. I've got a whole stack of books back at my house. All we have to do is read them and then come up with our own solution, one that we think will work ... and since our subconsciouses will be bound to believe in them, then obviously, the antidotes will work."

Jill had the feeling nothing was going to change the desire she felt whenever she was with Remy, but she was willing—no, anxious, actually—to put it to the test. She regarded Remy fondly. "That logic is so brilliantly convoluted, I'd almost think I'd come up with it myself," she teased.

"Of course," Remy drawled with a confident shrug. "Great minds think alike."

Jill looked into his eyes and found herself drawn into the beckoning depths. "So when do you want to do this research?" she asked softly.

Remy smiled back at her. "How about tonight?"

JILL FOLLOWED REMY into his house. It was easy to tell he had left in a hurry that morning. Although the dishes had been done, the kitchen tidied, the rest of his home still bore the remains of the impromptu party the night before. Folding chairs were set up here and there. Ashtrays needed emptying, floors needed sweeping, and throw pillows needed putting back in the usual places. She felt guilty for not helping him finish cleaning up. He had helped her and Kizzie tidy up Magnolia Place after the garden club left. "Look, Remy, before we do anything else, we've got to finish getting this place in order," she said.

He waved off her offer of help. "I can handle it later."

"Remy, I insist."

"Otherwise, you'll feel beholden to me, like you're taking advantage," he guessed unhappily.

"Right."

"Sugar, I hate to break it to you, but you're still in your party dress, and unlike your wonderful aunt, I don't keep any long frilly white aprons around."

Jill admitted to herself she was dying to get out of the frilly sundress. "So give me something else to wear," she said practically, "and then we'll vacuum and straighten up. Then we can put on a pot of coffee and come up with our own bound-to-work antidote."

"Sure you're up to all that after the day you put in?" Remy asked, obviously recalling her falling asleep, curled up on his sofa, the evening before.

Jill recalled waking to find herself wrapped in his arms, her head against his chest.

Fighting a flush, she pointed out, "Remy, it's only 8:00 p.m. We've got time to do this all tonight. Besides, I don't have anything else to do this evening." And, despite the risks involved in such a venture, she didn't want to spend the evening alone. She wanted to spend it with Remy.

"Okay." He shrugged, his sable eyes gleaming with a peculiarly determined light. "But I get to change, too."

He came back with a starched button-down oxford in pale yellow and plain white sweatpants with a drawstring waist for her. He had tossed his tie and jacket, left the light blue shirt on and put on a pair of jeans. He looked infinitely more comfortable—sexier, too. Just looking at him, Jill felt her pulse race. Finding an antidote to negate her feelings for him was going to be a lot harder than Remy Beauregard thought, she acknowledged silently. Particularly since she was no longer sure she wanted the antidote to work.

"This okay?" He held up his selections for her approval.

"It's great." Jill slipped off to change. His bathroom smelled of his piney after-shave, which in turn reminded her of the way he smelled when they were up close and personal.

Telling herself to hurry it up, she finished dressing, then studied herself in the mirror. The shirt was too big, of course, but it was a good color on her. Her hair looked great. Her cheeks were flushed, and her eyes were a little too bright to make anyone believe this was going to be just a casual evening between two people who had sort of become friends.

Nothing is going to happen tonight that I don't want to happen, Jill told her reflection in the mirror. The question was, what did she want to happen? And why did her heart race so whenever the question came up?

Taking her dress, slip, stockings and heels, she padded barefoot back out to the living room. Remy had already straightened it. She followed the sound of the vacuum cleaner and discovered he was almost finished cleaning the den. "I thought you were going to wait for me to help." Jill shouted to be heard above the machine, as she began collecting ashtrays.

"I am." Remy grinned and pointed to the kitchen. "You get to wash and dry all the ashtrays."

Ten minutes later, they were done. Remy and Jill sat down at the kitchen table with a carafe of coffee and a huge stack of books on Cajun folklore, folk medicine, aroma therapy, herbal therapy and love potions.

For the next hour they were absorbed in their reading. "Well, here's one that might work," Jill said eventually.

"Oh, yeah?" Remy looked up. "You actually found an aphrodisiac antidote?"

"Not exactly. It's a potion that's supposed to promote celibacy."

"Ohhhhh, nooooo, sugar." Remy pushed back his chair and stalked to the refrigerator. He returned with what was left of the praline cheesecake and two forks.

Jill grinned and they went back to reading. "Some of these ingredients for love potions don't sound half bad," Jill said, after a while. "Listen to what's in this one recipe. Vanilla extract, nutmeg, honey, red wine..."

"Some of them sound pretty terrible, too," Remy acknowledged as they split the last bite of cheesecake. "What is vervain anyway?"

"No idea." Jill frowned as she read a footnote at the bottom of the page. "It also says some of these herbs are potentially poisonous if taken in large doses."

Remy looked immediately concerned. "Then we'll stay away from all those," he said.

"Agreed."

They studied some more. "Have you noticed there are many more recipes for love potions than antidotes?" Jill asked with a frown.

Remy nodded. Silence fell between them. Finally he kicked back in his chair, propped his forearms on the table and offered, "Well, we could do what Madame Rousseau did. Cook up a love potion that we think'll work to enhance our feelings for each other, and then sour it with something really awful."

"Or," Jill said slowly, "we could cook up some potion that symbolizes all that's wrong with our relationship."

Remy snapped his fingers. "Got it."

"What?"

He sat forward in his chair. "I'm Louisiana and you're New York, right?"

"Right," Jill said slowly, her pulse beginning a slow heavy beat.

"So what's more Cajun than hot sauce?" He went to the cupboard and came back with a bottle of Tabasco sauce. "And what's more New York than..." His eyes met hers. He waited for Jill to fill in the blanks.

"I don't know." Jill groped around for a solution. "Street-vendor hot dogs with the works?"

"Hmmm," Remy said with a grin. "A love potion in the form of solid food. That would certainly be unusual."

"Well, cheesecake is pretty popular, too," Jill added, propping her chin on her elbow, "but I don't think I could bear to mix cheesecake with hot sauce."

"On a street-vendor hot dog it might work, though," Remy said, "and it wouldn't taste half bad, either."

Jill frowned, looking at her notes. "I still think we should have a drinkable antidote, too," she said.

"And we should prepare and imbibe the potions at midnight, under a full moon, if at all possible," Remy said, glancing at the notes he had made.

A full moon sounded very romantic.

Jill pushed her chair back and went to his kitchen window. "We're out of luck. That moon is only three-quarters, Remy."

He followed her to the window, and looked out at the evening sky. "So we'll make do," he said with a shrug as she turned to face him. "When do you want to cook up these potions?"

"I don't know." Jill bit her lip. They could do it tonight, but then that would take away all the reasons she had for being with him, particularly since the re-wiring was also done. Hoping he couldn't see through her as easily as she feared he could, she said, "How about tomorrow night? I think I need to study the books a little more."

He nodded agreeably, seemingly mesmerized by the dark blue hue of her eyes. "We really want it to work," he said softly, giving her a slow, sexy smile.

"Yes," Jill agreed as a peculiar melting sensation drifted through her from head to toe. "We do."

The next thing she knew she was in his arms, his mouth locked on hers. His tongue thrust inside her mouth, parrying deep, parrying soft. The need to surrender to him, to this, swept through her in undulating waves.

His kiss was possessive, his touch full of a need and yearning so strong, her whole body trembled in response and the last of her cautious resolve fled. His hands swept down her hips and caught her against him. She moved against him, wholly lost in the splendor of the moment.

Remy couldn't get enough of her. He had wanted her all day, from the first moment he had laid eyes on her. Kissing her in front of the entire garden club had been sweet torture. Just as this was torture, too.

Jill had a feeling they were getting in over their heads here. And a part of her, a newly discovered reckless part, didn't care. She wanted him to unbutton her shirt, and he did. She wanted him to unhook her bra, and he did that, too. He cupped her breasts in his hands, and caressed the nipples into tight, aching buds. She unbuttoned his shirt and pressed her breasts against the hair-whorled solidness of his chest, kissing him all the while, until she thought she would go wild with the unassuaged ache deep inside her.

With a groan, Remy broke off the kiss and buried his face in her hair. "Jill—"

Jill drew back and met his eyes. Tomorrow, perhaps, she would regret this, but she knew she couldn't walk away tonight without regretting it, too. Potion or no, she and Remy were meant to be together. She knew it in the deepest recesses of her soul. She lifted his hand and pressed a kiss into his palm. "Listen to me, Remy. Right now, there is nowhere else I'd rather be."

That was all Remy needed to hear. He swept her into his arms and carried her to his bed. He followed her down onto the soft hand-quilted coverlet that still bore the imprint of their bodies from the night before. Framing her face with his hands, he kissed her thoroughly, until she was breathless and limp with longing, until she arched up against him, every inch of her aching with the need to be touched, loved, adored, as only he could adore her.

They might not have the future, Remy thought, but they had now...tonight...and he was determined to make the most of it. He brought her close for a long, luxurious kiss. Impatient with the barriers between them, he kicked off his jeans and his briefs, and helped her take off the sweats and the tiny triangle of white lace. She was beautiful and sweet and silky with need. The moments spun out timelessly as he caressed every rose-scented inch of her, first with his hands, and then with his lips.

Jill arched against him helplessly as he sent her into a whirlpool of dizzying sensation. She clasped his shoulders, lifting him closer, gasping as he moved over her, gasping again as he entered her. Helpless, drowning in her own pleasure, she let him take her where he wanted, let him thrust and then touch, thrust and then touch, until she thought she would lose her mind, until they were half-on, half-off the bed. Her arms around his shoulders, her legs wrapped around his waist, she held on tight as he kissed her again and again and again, holding back, giving a little more, then holding back again.

No one had ever made love to her like this before. She hadn't even been able to imagine. "Remy," she whispered, slipping a hand between them, caressing, too. Her touch took him over the edge, and then he was thrusting into her blindly, passionately, until both were shuddering in response.

Afterward, they clung together. Shaking. Throbbing. Wanting more. Remy groaned, and realizing they were still positioned somewhat precariously on the bed, turned and lifted her back up onto the pillows. He draped his body over hers, cradling her in rugged male warmth. Jill lay with her head against his shoulder. He felt good, she thought. He felt so damn good. With Remy, there were no inhibitions. Nothing off-limits. Everything was sensual and easy and wonderful. So incredibly, incredibly wonderful. She could get used to this living in the moment.

Leaning over her, he smoothed the tangled hair from her face. "I have wanted to make love to you for so damn long," he whispered with a soft, sexy smile. And then lowering his mouth to hers, he started all over again.

They made love through the night. Jill was exhausted when dawn came, but no less confused. She was afraid she was falling in love with Remy, deeply irrevocably in love with him. At the same time, she feared a long-term relationship with him would never work. And a long-term relationship, and not a fling, was what she wanted with him.

"You look troubled, sugar," Remy observed softly. Early-morning sunshine filtered into the room, illuminating them both in a gentle glow.

"Making love to you last night should have settled things between us," Jill said. "It should have shown us a way to end it or... or... satisfied our curiosity about each other to the point where we could just get on with our lives and not be so obsessed with each other."

"But it didn't do any of that, did it?" Remy guessed slowly. Instead, making love with Jill had filled his heart with her, filled it in ways that he knew he was never going to get over. And that meant that walking away from Jill when the end came—as she kept insisting it must—was going to be much more painful than he had anticipated.

"No," Jill said with a soft, sad sigh, "making love with you last night didn't clarify anything." Instead, it had made her incessant, irrational longing for him worse. Because now she wanted him heart and soul, in ways that could never be.

They were two opposites. She was career-driven. He worked because it was necessary to eat, not because he needed it to breathe. He took inordinate pleasure in simple things she barely noticed. He lived each day without worrying about the future. Jill lived as much in the future as she did in the present. He was Cajun to his bones. She was brought up to be a Southern lady, but these days felt more like a New Yorker, born and bred. Her work was in the city. He loved the country. So where did that leave them? And why couldn't she be less wedded to complex long-term relationships and simply enjoy a fling, like any other reasonable, rational, consenting adult?

She looked over at him and saw he was grinning that smug grin of his again, as if he knew, despite all the evidence to the contrary, that things were bound to work out. "You've got no right to be looking so happy, Remy. This is a real problem." How was she going to go back to New York feeling like she did?

"Confused, aren't you?" he prodded in a low, gravelly tone.

"And then some," she admitted.

He held her closer, smoothing her hair with the flat of his hand. "Well, we're supposed to cook up our antidotes tonight," Remy said, his warm breath sending shivers down her spine as he whispered in her ear. "Maybe that'll help."

Jill cuddled closer, her face pressed against his bare chest. The tenderness of his embrace conveyed a yearning that was getting out of control, a yearning that overwhelmed her even as it seduced. She wanted him, had wanted this, but now that the dawn had come, she was scared to find herself opening up to the potential for hurt again.

For so long, she had trusted no one, let no one get close. Remy was tearing down the barriers to her heart one by one, making her really believe there could be more to life than work, family and friends. Making her believe there could be love—passionate, terrifying, wonderful, beautiful love in her life.

She drew back to look at him. There was no clue as to what he was thinking or feeling in his face. "You really think taking another antidote will work in negating our feelings for each other?" she asked skeptically.

No, Remy thought, *I don't, but it's an excuse to be together again.* He had a feeling that if he didn't have a solid "worthwhile" excuse for them to be together tonight, Jill might just cut and run while she tried to sort things out. And he didn't want that.

His glance was deliberately enigmatic as he bent to kiss her brow lightly. "It seems to me, sugar, cooking up our own homemade antidotes is worth a try. There's always the chance it won't work, but then there's the chance it will, and if it does, then we won't feel this way anymore."

Jill held her breath, wishing for once Remy would tell her more of what was on his mind and in his heart, instead of behaving in his usual happy-go-lucky, I'll-take-what-life-hands-me way.

"You still want to reverse the potion?" she asked warily, aware her heart was pounding heavily in her chest as she waited for his reply.

Remy studied her carefully. "Don't you?"

Chapter Eleven

Jill didn't know what to say. The reasons why they shouldn't be together, couldn't be together, were all still valid. Yet the night of passionate lovemaking had changed her. She wanted more out of life than she had a day or even a week ago. She wanted more than work; she wanted marriage, children—the works. But she didn't want them with just anyone. She wanted them with Remy.

But she also knew she was moving too quickly. Her failed marriage to Jake had made her wary of making another mistake. Maybe she should follow Remy's example and just live in the present.

He was still waiting for an answer.

"Do you or do you not want the potion reversed?" Remy asked her softly.

Jill wasn't sure what Remy wanted her to say. There was no clue in the impassive expression on his face. "Part of me doesn't believe in potions," she said slowly. "You know that. But there's another part, a deeply buried, primal superstitious part that does. And I wouldn't want to think that what we shared last night was due to anything but . . . natural feelings."

Remy grinned, looking as if he felt the exact same way. "So we're in agreement?" he asked cheerfully. "We work together tonight to counter the love potions we imbibed?"

Jill nodded, her spirits rising once again as her doubts faded. As far as she was concerned, any reason for them to be together was a good reason. Besides, as she had said to him the night before, what they would be doing was bound to be so silly, it couldn't help but be fun. "What time do you want to meet?" Jill asked.

Remy shrugged. "Seven okay with you?"

"COUNT ME IN," Elanore said after Jill had explained her plan over lunch.

"Me, too," Frieda said.

"I think we'd all make excellent roommates," Maizie concurred.

"Now all I have to do is ask my aunt," Jill said with a smile.

As she had hoped, Hildy was thrilled with the idea, too. "When could they move in?" she asked.

"Elanore said she can move in late next week, if you're ready for her."

"That would be wonderful," Hildy said. "Though of course it means you and I won't be together again, Jill." She looked a little sad about that.

Jill understood her aunt's melancholy. She missed seeing her aunt on a daily basis, too. "The offer is still good for you to come and live with me in New York."

Her aunt shook her head. "I'll visit. I promise. Just as soon as my ankle is strong enough and I've got my arm out of this cast. The city is great to visit, but I belong in the country, Jill. I belong in the South.''

"I know." Jill fluffed her aunt's pillows. "I understand, I really do."

"So, what did you do last night?" Hildy asked as Jill moved about the hospital room, tidying up.

Jill paused to better arrange the vases of flowers displayed on the windowsill. "I went to Remy's for a while."

Hildy regarded her curiously. "Something brewing between the two of you?"

If you only knew, Jill thought, and barely managed to suppress a blush. "We're, um, trying to figure out a way to cook up an antidote to the love potions we drank."

"Oh, really?" Hildy looked down her nose at Jill. "Why would you want to do that?"

Jill shrugged and continued acting a lot more nonchalant than she felt. "I don't know. It seemed like a good idea at the time?"

Hildy regarded Jill cagily. "You have feelings for him, don't you, dear?"

As usual, Aunt Hildy saw far too much. Jill went back to arranging and rearranging the vases of flowers. "For all the good it will do either of us," she replied lightly.

"The two of you could be together," Hildy insisted.

Jill knew there was no way she was giving up being head writer on "The Brave and the Beautiful." "Not long-term."

Hildy pressed a button beside her and raised the head on her hospital bed. "Don't let a good man like Remy get away, Jill," Hildy admonished. "If you do, you'll regret it the rest of your life."

I might very well do that, Jill thought, *but I don't have any choice. I can't give up my job in New York, and I can't ask him to move there.* "Remy is a true Cajun, Aunt Hildy. Louisiana is in his blood. He would never be happy anywhere else. I can't ask him to give up his business and his life here. It wouldn't be fair." Just like it wouldn't be fair of Remy to ask her to give up her work, Jill thought.

"You care about him that much?" Hildy said gently.

That much and more, Jill thought.

Hildy began to fidget in her bed. "Jill, darling, would you be a dear and do an errand for me?"

Jill smiled, glad to concentrate on something else. "Anything. You know that."

"Please go to the market down the street and get a Sunday paper for me. And if it's not too much trouble, a basket of fruit and a fresh box of chocolates. Several of my friends from the garden club are going to visit me tonight and I'd like to have something here to offer guests when they stop in to see me."

REMY PASSED JILL as she was on her way out of the hospital parking lot. He stopped just inside the entrance and rolled down his car window. She rolled down hers. "Great minds think alike, again," he teased, wondering how he had ever gotten along before Jill came into his life. "Were you just up to see Hildy?"

"Yes." Jill waved a paper in her hand and beamed him a radiant smile. "She gave me a list of errands to do for her, as per usual." Her dark blue eyes sparkling, Jill asked, "Are you going up to see her?"

He nodded.

"Well, don't rush off," Jill advised. "I'll be back in twenty minutes or so."

"I'll wait for you," Remy promised.

Jill waved and drove off. Remy parked his car in the lot. It was going to be strange when Jill went back to New York and he no longer had the chance to see her every day. But he wouldn't think about that now. Thinking that way... worrying about the future... was definitely not Cajun.

He would concentrate on the present, he decided as he strolled down the hall to Hildy's hospital room. The door was opened only slightly, the television on. Afraid she might be dozing, Remy peered into the room. Instead of seeing Hildy asleep in her bed, he saw her wide-awake and *standing!*

Amazement turned to anger. "What are you doing up and walking around on that ankle?" he demanded. Being fiercely independent was one thing, he thought, taking foolish chances quite another.

Hildy turned around with a start. Her cheeks flushed a rosy pink as she continued to grip the edge of her bed with her right hand. "Remy, you scared me!"

"I'll bet." Remy closed the door behind him and hurried to her side. "And you didn't answer my question." He looked down at her left ankle, which was still wrapped in an Ace bandage. "Dr. Destrehan said you weren't to put any weight on it until the pain went away," he scolded.

"The pain went away the same time the swelling did, several days ago," Hildy admitted reluctantly. "I didn't let on because I didn't want Jill to leave."

"Because you'd miss her," Remy said sympathetically, as Hildy continued to walk slowly back and forth, testing her once-sprained ankle, and apparently finding it more than fine.

"No," Hildy corrected. "I didn't tell anyone because if Jill left then you and Jill would never finish falling in love!"

Her words struck a nerve in Remy, maybe because he wanted the same thing. Nevertheless, he couldn't give Hildy false hope. "Whether either of us like it or not, Hildy, your niece has a career in New York," he lectured sternly. "And I have a life here."

"You could move to New York."

Yes, I could, Remy thought, but Jill hasn't asked me. And he wasn't going to trail after her like some lovesick teenager with no life of his own. "I have a business here, Hildy," he reminded her, hovering over the woman anxiously as she shuffled back and forth.

"So move your business to New York," Hildy advised.

Remy tried to picture himself in New York City. He couldn't do it. He tried to picture himself with Jill in New York City. That was a little easier, but still not all that comfortable. And he had gotten to a point in his life where he enjoyed being comfortable with his surroundings. "It's not that simple, Hildy," Remy said slowly.

Hildy quirked a dissenting brow. "Isn't it?"

"I admit I'm a little smitten with Jill," Remy said. "But realistically, the most Jill and I can hope for right now is a few days or evenings of romance." Anything more . . . well, they'd just have to see.

"Oh, don't be so darn Cajun!" Hildy exclaimed in complete exasperation. "This isn't one of those things you just have to accept! There's no reason for you to be at all nonchalant about this, Remy Beauregard!" Hildy shook an admonishing finger at Remy as her voice rose. "If you want Jill even half as much as I think you do, then I darn well expect you to put up a fight!"

JILL HEARD the loud, emotional voices coming from her aunt's room when she reached the nurses' station. She couldn't make out much of what was being said, but she heard her aunt shouting Remy's name, and the word *fight!* Not sure what was happening down there, only knowing she had to stop it, she rushed toward the door, her heels *clattering* on the polished linoleum floor. She knocked hurriedly, then not waiting for formal permission to enter, pushed the door to Hildy's hospital room open with the flat of her palm. Remy was standing next to her aunt . . . who was also standing!

Upon seeing Jill, both Remy's and Hildy's faces turned pale. Hildy began to swoon. Fortunately for them all, Remy caught her before she could slip to the floor.

Feeling so upset, her heart seemed as though it would leap right out of her body, Jill slapped a hand to her chest. "What's going on here?" she cried.

Hildy pressed her hand to her forehead. Her paleness faded. "Remy, darling, you're right," Hildy announced with theatrical aplomb, as her cheeks glowed a brilliant pink. "I shouldn't try to walk on this sprained ankle of mine, even if the swelling has practically disappeared." Hildy looked up at Remy so sweetly, Jill was instantly suspicious. "Could you be a dear and help me get back into bed?"

Jill took a closer look at her aunt. Was she seeing things or was Hildy actually batting her eyelashes at Remy? And why was Remy giving Hildy that mock chastising look? The same kind he gave her when they were pulling something over on someone!

"Certainly, Hildy, dear," Remy replied saccharinely as he turned back the sheets on the hospital bed. He guided Hildy around until she was seated on the side of the bed. He helped settle her in, then drew the covers up to her waist.

Jill put down her packages and continued watching them both. As far as she was concerned, Hildy and Remy both looked far too innocent to be believed. Jill propped her hands on her hips. "What was going on in here just now?" Jill demanded.

Hildy and Remy exchanged glances. They shrugged. Neither spoke.

"I could hear the two of you arguing three rooms away!"

Hildy's cheeks turned a little pinker. Avoiding Jill's glance, she continued smoothing the covers on her bed. "It was nothing, dear. Remy was just trying to talk a little sense into me."

Remy looked at Hildy rather pointedly. "Did I succeed?" he asked dryly.

Again, Hildy didn't answer.

"Talk sense into you about what?" Jill asked impatiently.

"My ankle," Hildy finally explained. For the first time since Jill had entered the room, Hildy looked directly at Jill. "I wanted to try to walk on it, and Remy said I had to wait until I had Dr. Destrehan's permission."

Another beat of silence followed. "And that's it?" Jill queried. She was sure it wasn't.

Hildy gestured helplessly. "What else could it be?"

That was just it. Jill didn't know. But she could swear by the looks on both their faces, something was up. She didn't like being the odd man out.

Remy looked at his watch. "Well, I've got to be going," he said. "One of my regular customers called—they've got a short in the kitchen, and I promised I'd be out to fix it right away. I'll be back to see you tomorrow, Hildy." Remy bent to kiss Hildy goodbye. "We'll talk more then," he promised Hildy.

Again, Jill had the feeling something was going on, but it was also clear the two of them weren't about to share it with her. She caught Remy's arm before he could leave. For once, not caring if her aunt saw or not, Jill asked, "Are we still on for tonight?" She hoped his work wasn't going to interfere with that. Although, being a workaholic herself, she could hardly complain if it did.

...e're on for tonight," Remy said with a sexy ...I'll be done with that job long before then." ...ssed Jill's cheek, too, gave Hildy another hu- ...ously censuring look, then ducked out the door.

Jill picked up the Sunday paper and carried it over to her aunt. "I suppose you're not going to tell me what's going on between the two of you," Jill said to Hildy.

"Nope. But you can tell me what's going on between you and Remy. What was all that about tonight? You didn't tell me earlier that you two had a date this evening, just that you were together last night!"

Jill was loathe to call it a date, even though she knew that was exactly what it was. "Remy and I are going to cook up our antidotes to the love potions Kizzie and his friend Gator gave us," she said casually.

"Why would you want to do that?"

Because it's an excuse to be together, and probably—hopefully—make love again, Jill thought. Not about to admit that to her aunt, for fear of what Hildy would make of it, Jill shrugged. "It just seems like a good idea."

"Oh, I see. Remy's kiss at the garden club meeting yesterday really got to you, didn't it?" Hildy teased.

Jill felt her own cheeks heat and knew they were as pink as Hildy's had been when she had first walked into her aunt's hospital room.

Not nearly as much as Remy's lovemaking, Jill thought. But it was true. Remy made her feel as though she were the only woman in the world for him. And she felt the same way about him.

"I am not discussing Remy's kisses unless you tell me what you two were up to," Jill bargained.

"Then I guess we'll just have to forego that interesting discussion, won't we?" Hildy said, not the least bit nonplussed. "So what do you want to talk about?"

"My plans for the upcoming week. Is there anything you want me to do for you while I'm in town?" Jill asked. "You know I want to stay until everything is settled and your ankle is healed well enough for you to be released from the hospital—"

Abruptly, Hildy looked so uncomfortable, Jill lost track of what she was saying. Immediately concerned, she leaned forward urgently. "What is it, Aunt Hildy? Are you in pain?"

"No, dear, I'm fine." Hildy cleared her throat. She nervously patted her ample chest, and then, after a moment, seemed to regain her composure. "About Remy..."

"Yes?"

"And your plans for this evening?" Hildy continued.

"What about them?" Jill said, wishing her aunt would stick to discussing one subject at a time.

Hildy sent her an admonishing glance. "It's not like you to let anything or anyone you want get away from you. If I were you, Jill, I'd think twice about cooking up that antidote."

REMY ARRIVED PROMPTLY at seven, carrying a bag of charcoal in one hand and a grocery bag in the other.

Jill could tell he had recently showered and shaved. She told herself it was because he had just come from a job, but she knew better. She knew it was because he was anticipating making love to her again, once they saw their antidotes didn't work, and he wanted to be at his sensual, sexy best.

"You usually buy New York hot dogs on the street, don't you?" he asked as he set everything down in her kitchen.

Jill tried hard not to notice how crisply ironed his white oxford-cloth shirt was, how snug and sparkling clean his jeans. "Yes."

"Well, I don't have a street-vendor cooking rig, but figure we can make do with Hildy's grill out back."

Jill grinned at the thought Remy had put into this. Like her, he seemed to want everything to be perfect. "You got the Cajun hot sauce, I see," she observed drolly.

"As well as every fixing imaginable," he said as he finished emptying his bag. He folded the grocery sack and turned to her. "What about you?"

Jill ignored the appreciative way his glance roved her short, straight-skirted light blue shirtdress before returning to her face. She pointed to the stove. "I've been cooking up my own antidote all evening," Jill admitted. When she hadn't been trying on every single outfit she'd brought with her, in a desperate search for something appropriately sexy but country casual to wear.

Remy wrinkled his nose in the direction of the stove. "Is that what smells like potpourri?"

Jill nodded, aware the mixture was probably a little too fruity for his taste. "Right now, it's some herbs and vanilla and pureed fruit simmering in a little water, but I'm going to cool it, and then add it to the wine."

Remy grabbed her around the waist and pulled her close. "It's not a celibacy potion, is it?"

Jill tingled every place they touched. "I told you I wouldn't do that."

"Just checking," he said.

"It's a simple love potion, to which I plan to add a lot of sour lemon."

"Oh. Sounds more drinkable than the vinegar laced peppermint tea Madame Rousseau served us."

"Let's hope so," Jill said.

They grinned at each other, both of them obviously looking forward to the evening ahead. And as they looked into each other's eyes, it wasn't hard for Jill to see why Hildy and the other ladies in the garden club were all so fond of Remy. He had a heart as big as Louisiana and a self-deprecating quality she liked. Unlike most of the men she met in New York, he didn't take himself too seriously. Nor did he ever undercut anyone else or not take them seriously enough.

Remy smiled at her. "While you finish in here, I'll set up the grill outside."

"So how was the rest of your day?" Jill asked twenty minutes later as she brought out a tray full of condiments and the cooling love potion and joined him on the steps that led down to the backyard. The charcoal was almost all white.

"Busy. Yours?"

"Actually a little boring," Jill admitted. She frowned, as she thought about the lonely hours after she had left the hospital, before Remy had arrived. "I'm not used to having so much free time on my hands." Usually she filled every spare minute with work.

Remy plucked a dark hair from her cheek and tucked it behind her ear. "You only had a few hours," he chided.

"Yes," Jill said with a sigh. "But normally I work seven days a week."

Remy shook his head as he got up and added their hot dogs to the grill. "I don't think I could live like that."

"Too much work makes Remy a dull boy?" Jill teased.

"A tired and sad and lonely boy," he corrected, sitting down beside her. "Not to say I haven't had weeks like that. I have. But most of the time I need my weekends to recharge my batteries and spend time with friends."

Jill had lived that way once, too. When she was married.

Feeling suddenly restless, she got up to turn the hot dogs. The fire Remy had built was very hot, and the hot dogs were cooking quickly. She put a package of foil-wrapped buns on the grate, and a small skillet of sauerkraut. Almost immediately, the kraut began to sizzle.

"Speaking of friends...how did your aunt take the idea about living with her friends?" Remy asked.

Jill smiled, glad Hildy's reaction had been everything she'd hoped for and more. "She loved it."

"That must be a relief to you."

Jill shrugged as she moved restlessly back and forth beside the grill. "It is and it isn't. I'm still going to miss her. If nothing else, her fall made me realize that our time together may be running out. I don't want to waste it, Remy. And yet at the same time, I can't move back here. I've got a contract with the network and the show for the next two years, and an obligation to the people there."

Remy got up to stand beside her. "So visit Hildy a little more often," he proposed gently.

"I notice you're not telling me to give up my career," she remarked lightly, as she gave the kraut another whirl.

"I'd never do that, Jill."

As he looked down at her, Jill felt a bond growing between them. The kind of bond married people had. The thought should have disconcerted her, made her wary and nervous. It didn't. Refusing to analyze what that meant, Jill looked back down at the food. "The hot dogs are ready, Remy."

Jill transferred the cooked food from the grill to a serving tray. Remy carried it up to a wrought-iron table on the veranda.

"And now...the moment of truth," Remy announced dramatically as he doused each New York-style dog liberally with Cajun hot sauce.

"Do New York and Louisiana mix?" Jill asked.

They each took a bite at the same time. Jill had never tasted anything hotter or spicier in her life. It

was also good . . . in a very different way. "I can't believe it. I actually like this," she said.

"Me, too," Remy said. Their eyes met and he
grinned cheerfully. "So much for this working as an
antidote to Kizzie's potion or Gator's aphrodisiac," he
said.

"Ah, yes, but we still have the potion that I cooked
up," Jill said.

Remy looked at the decanter. "You want to drink
it?"

Jill touched the side of the glass. "I think it's still
too hot. We're going to have to wait awhile." The
truth was, Jill didn't want to drink it. She didn't want
their excuse to be together wiped out or the evening to
end, or the magic between them to disappear. And
though the chance of their own antidote "working"
was extremely remote, it was still a chance she didn't
want to take. Nor, to her relief, did Remy seem in any
rush to "end" things between them.

Remy pointed to the sky. "See it? A falling star."

"Oh, yeah," Jill said softly, watching it speed
across the black velvet of the sky, and the night became even more magical than it already was.

Remy drew her to her feet and led her to the edge of
the porch. "Time to make a wish," he said.

*I wish I may, I wish I might, I wish I'd fall in love
with Remy tonight,* Jill thought. *And,* she added, *I
wish he would fall in love with me.*

Did that count as two wishes? Or just one?

Remy looked at her, his own thoughts hidden. "Did
you make one?"

Jill nodded, her senses in a riot as he draped a possessive arm about her waist. "Yes."

"Me, too," he said softly, meaningfully.

Jill looked at him and knew she was going to miss him terribly when she left. "Was yours for the present or the future?" she asked softly.

"Both. What about yours?"

She thought about love and wished it could last forever. "Both," she said quietly.

He escorted her back to their seat. "What would you like your future to be like?"

Jill settled next to him on the plump cushions of the wicker settee. He put his arm around her and she crossed her legs at the knee, letting hers nudge his just a little bit. "I'm not sure," she said.

Remy leaned over and pressed a kiss in her hair. "I know what I want. To marry and have a family."

Jill swallowed. That was something she probably would not be able to give Remy. Not unless he moved to New York to be with her, and she frankly could just not see him doing that.

"What do you want?" Remy asked as he traced lazy patterns on her shoulder with his fingertips.

Jill leaned back and closed her eyes. She breathed in the spicy scent of his cologne and the clean soap-and-water fragrance of his skin. "For my aunt to be well again, and happy with all her friends."

"That's for Hildy," he corrected gently, taking her chin in his hand. "What do you want for you, Jill?" he asked as her eyes opened and she met his searching gaze.

"For the show to continue to be a success," Jill said, as her heart began a slow, languid beat.

Remy shook his head. "That's work," he said, as he dragged a thumb across her lower lip. "I meant in your personal life."

"I don't know," Jill said as his thumb moved to her cheek, her jaw, creating frissons of sensations on her skin. "I don't let myself dream about a personal life."

"Then it's time that changed, Jill," Remy said.

Taking her into his arms, he kissed her until she began to realize he was right, until she began to dream of marrying him in front of the entire garden club and all their family and friends. She kissed him until she was dizzy with the taste and touch and feel of him.

She opened her arms to him; she opened her heart. She gave him everything he needed, everything he asked for, letting him know with every look and touch and kiss that she really did care about him, that she really did love him, even though they hadn't yet said the words, hadn't dared say the words....

Remy waited until he could stand it no longer, then carried her upstairs and eased her down onto her canopy bed. Dispensing with their clothes was easy. Putting a rein on his feelings was not. "I want you," he murmured against her throat. "You can't imagine how much I want you, Jill." *More than life itself.*

A shudder ran through her. "Oh, Remy," Jill murmured back tenderly. "I want you, too. So much," she whispered. "So very much...."

"Not just tonight," Remy said, bracing his arms on either side of her and looking deep into her eyes. "But forever..."

Jill had been waiting to hear those words for a lifetime. "Oh, Remy," she whispered back. "Oh, Remy..." *I love you, too,* she thought. *So very much.* He kissed her again, deeply this time, using pressure and tenderness a thousand different ways, until she moaned soft and low in her throat, needing and wanting so much more than simple kisses and caresses from him.

Yielding as he spread his hands across her abdomen, she guided her hips up to his. His body shuddered with barely leashed longing, and then they were as one.

Jill moaned softly as a feeling of fulfillment centered in her heart and radiated outward in hot, mesmerizing waves. She knew this was what life was all about. No one but Remy had ever loved her like this or held her like this, and she knew instinctively that no one else ever would. Not with this intensity. Not with this much love...

Afterward, Jill said drowsily, "We forgot to take the antidote I cooked up." *Even though I didn't really want to take it, may never want to take it...*

"Forget the antidote," Remy said gruffly as he covered her body with his once again. His lips moved steadily down her throat, to the accelerating pulse. His sable eyes were dark with pleasure, his breath warm and fragrant against the heat of her skin. "This is all we need, Jill, all we'll ever need."

And as he kissed her again, Jill believed him.

Chapter Twelve

"I never thought a sprained ankle was a lucky thing," Jill said bright and early the next morning. "But it certainly has turned out to be lucky for us."

"What do you mean?" A towel wrapped around his waist, Remy emerged from her bathroom. The two of them had stayed in her shower until the water ran cold. Looking at her clad in nothing but the thick pink-and-white terry-cloth robe, Remy was tempted to drag her right back in again.

"If not for Aunt Hildy's sprained ankle, I wouldn't have had to stay in Louisiana." Jill crossed the distance between them lithely, slipped her arms around his waist and leaned her head on his shoulder. "And if Aunt Hildy hadn't had to stay in the hospital because of her sprained ankle, I wouldn't have met you."

Remy felt a flash of guilt. Had he known earlier, about Jill's con man father, and how sensitive she was to the idea of being "conned" into anything—even good-naturedly—he never would have allowed Hildy to put one over on Jill, even for a slight time. He had the feeling Jill would go ballistic if she found out her aunt had been faking, even just a tad, in order to help Jill and Remy's romance along.

He had to get this straightened out right away.

He had to talk to Hildy.

He tightened his arms around Jill and held her even closer, threading his hands through her hair. Jill lifted her face to his. They indulged in another long, leisurely kiss.

The phone rang and they drew apart reluctantly. Jill picked up the receiver.

"Hi, Patty," Jill said. She turned to Remy and mouthed, "My assistant in New York," then focused her attention back to the caller. "What's up?"

Remy watched as Jill frowned. "You're not kidding, are you?" Her dark blue eyes clouded with disappointment. "They really want me there tomorrow afternoon?" She paused again, frowning. "That means I'd have to fly in, in the morning."

His heart twisting painfully, Remy gathered his clothes and began to dress. He hadn't expected it to be over so soon.

Jill hung up. Remy shrugged on his jeans. "Problems?" he asked as he zipped his jeans and reached for his shirt.

Jill nodded, her voice brisk and businesslike. "The network is wooing a major advertiser. They want me at a meeting tomorrow afternoon, to pitch the upcoming story lines for 'The Brave and the Beautiful.' There's a dinner afterward at Tavern On The Green. I'm expected to attend that, too."

You knew this was coming, Remy told himself firmly. *You knew all along she was going to have to leave.*

The only problem was he had lied to himself when he'd told himself he could handle it. He was beginning to see letting her go was going to be a lot harder than he'd thought, if not damn near impossible.

Forcing himself to be as pragmatic as she was being, Remy forced a smile. "Sounds exciting," he drawled.

Jill tightened the belt on her robe and went to the vanity. She sat down and began dragging a comb through the damp ends of her hair. "It means I'll have to spend the afternoon writing the pitch, and then fly out first thing tomorrow."

Remy nodded as he finished buttoning his shirt and found his shoes. "Sounds reasonable."

Jill swiveled around on the vanity bench until she faced him. She lowered the comb to her lap. Her expression was both guarded and watchful, as if this were some kind of a test.

"You don't seem very upset," she said after a moment.

Remy strode closer. The sudden vulnerability in her dark blue eyes had him reaching for her. Taking her hand, he drew her to her feet and wrapped his arms around her. He felt her tremble as their bodies collided, saw the tears shimmering just beneath the surface of her eyes and knew this was just as hard for her as it was for him.

He drew a breath and held her close. "It's your job, Jill." He rested his cheek against her hair, breathing in the flowery scent of her, then drew back. Their glances collided. "More than that," he continued, "it's your life's work. Of course I understand."

Jill swallowed nervously, but her voice was strong as she asked, "Even if it means leaving you?"

Remy knew a lot was riding on his reply.

He took her into his arms once again. "This isn't the end of us, Jill." And as he said the words, he knew they were true. There were ways to work this out. He and Jill would find them, and he knew exactly how he would start.

His heart racing with the first of his plans, he bent his head and kissed her thoroughly, until she was limp and pliant against him. As Jill whispered his name, Remy lowered her to the bed, and began to make slow, thorough love to her. He didn't know precisely how much time Jill had left—this visit—but he wasn't going to waste a second of it.

"I FEEL TERRIBLE about leaving while Aunt Hildy is still in the hospital, even for a few days," Jill said two hours later, after the two of them had finished a leisurely breakfast.

"Don't worry about your aunt." In a hurry to set his secret plans in motion, Remy gulped the last of his chicory coffee, then set his cup on the counter. "I'll take care of her. And Elanore, Maizie and Frieda will visit and look in on her, too."

"I know. But I worry...."

Remy bent to kiss Jill thoroughly. "Don't." It was past time Hildy's ruse ended and his and Jill's future began, he thought. "I'll see you this evening," he promised as she walked him to the door. In the meantime, he had a very important errand to run.

"SO WHAT DO YOU THINK?" Remy asked an hour later as he showed Hildy the diamond ring he had purchased for Jill.

Hildy shook her head in open admiration. "It's beautiful, Remy." Her pale green eyes sparkling, she looked into his eyes. "Does it mean what I think it means?"

Remy nodded as he drew a chair up to the one Hildy was sitting in. "I'm going to ask her to marry me."

Morning sunlight streamed in through the blinds, illuminating them both. "What about all the problems?" Hildy asked, the youthful vitality in her face becoming all the more pronounced. "What about the two of you having jobs in two different states?"

Remy shrugged. "I figure if I can start a Beauregard Electric business here, I can start one in New York."

Hildy leaned forward in her chair and studied him like a protective mother hen. "You'd really do that for Jill, give up your home in Louisiana?"

She knew how much he loved it here.

So much, Remy thought, that Jill or no Jill he was still loathe to leave.

"Actually, I'm hoping I won't have to give up my house here entirely even after we marry, that we can keep it as a kind of Southern home base," Remy admitted.

"I always knew you were a clever young man," Hildy said with a wink.

"You think I'm doing the right thing?" He knew how skittish Jill was when it came to romance, yet he wanted Jill to know how he felt before she left for New York again. He wanted her to know they could have a future, and that he was willing to make whatever sacrifices that entailed. Hopefully, she would make some, too. He knew if she met him halfway on this that they could make their relationship work.

Hildy smiled as she predicted, "Jill is going to be very happy when she sees the ring. Furthermore, she's going to know she misjudged you from the very first."

Remy was sure Jill loved him, even though she hadn't come out and said the exact words yet; neither of them had. Nevertheless, this situation was going to require careful handling. And the first thing they had to deal with was Hildy's ankle, and the collusion he had been unwittingly drawn into the day before. He wanted no secrets between himself and Jill.

"Before I ask Jill to marry me, I want you to come clean with her, and let her know your ankle is all right, and that there's no longer any reason for her to worry about that," Remy said.

"It'll be a relief to do so," Hildy said as she scooted forward to the edge of the chair. Using the arm as leverage, she got slowly to her feet. "Now, about this proposal," she began as she slowly walked back and forth. "I want all the details. When, how and where are you going to ask that niece of mine to marry you?"

Remy grinned as he kept pace beside Hildy. Because she required no assistance, he offered none. "I'm glad you brought that up, Hildy, 'cause I think I could use your advice...."

JILL STEPPED OUT of the elevator and headed for Hildy's hospital room in a rush. She had so much to do today! The pitch to write, packing to do, a special dinner to prepare for her and Remy....

The sound of laughter from Hildy's room brought a smile to Jill's face. But the words she inadvertently overheard stopped her cold in her tracks.

"...Jill is not that hard to handle!" Remy was saying in his low, distinctly Southern voice.

"Until you came along, she was," Hildy said. "Oh, Remy, I am so pleased everything worked out the way I wanted."

"I couldn't have done it without you, and Kizzie," Remy admitted gratefully.

What did he mean he couldn't have done it without Hildy and Kizzie? Jill thought. Done what? He was talking as if the three of them had been involved in some sort of conspiracy.

"Kizzie did get things off to a sizzling start, didn't she?" Hildy murmured with a laugh.

A sizzling start! What the heck were they talking about? Jill wondered uneasily. Certainly nothing that involved her!

Remy chuckled, the low sexy sound of his voice drifting out from Hildy's hospital room and into the antiseptic-smelling hallway. "You know how the story goes...that Love Potion #5 works every time. At least," he teased, "it did for us."

Aunt Hildy and Remy laughed softly, intimately.

A flush started in Jill's chest, worked its way up through her neck and into her face. She was so embarrassed she could feel her ears burning, so stunned she couldn't seem to move at all. She couldn't believe she had actually allowed Remy and her aunt to reduce her to eavesdropping, and yet she couldn't seem to move away, either.

"Well, you just let me know if you need any more help with Jill, Remy," Hildy said confidently, "because where my darling niece is concerned, I'm all too willing to help stack the deck, if you know what I mean."

Remy chuckled again. "I surely do, Hildy, and thank you, really, for all your assistance. My wooing your niece probably would've happened either way, but your...insights...made it all the easier."

So they'd talked about her, too, Jill thought furiously.

Deciding she had heard more than enough, Jill rounded the corner, marched into her aunt's hospital room and then caught her breath at what she saw. Her Aunt Hildy was not in bed, a chair or the wheelchair. She was walking about the room without the assistance of a walker or even a cane. Hildy was walking as easily as if she had never sprained her ankle at all!

Seeing her, Remy and Hildy both went pale. Only today there was no attempt to fake a swoon, as there had been the day before. There was no time.

Remy abruptly shoved something small and square into his pocket. "How much of what we were just saying did you overhear?" he asked calmly.

He looked so nonchalant, Jill felt ill. What was it her con man father used to say? Lie, and if caught, lie again.

She couldn't believe she had been taken in by a ruthless charmer. She had grown up, watching her father operate, the first eight years of her life. She knew the signs . . . the way a man like that could get under a woman's skin without her even realizing it at all . . . and she had ignored them all. *Fool,* she deemed herself silently. *Idiot.* But that didn't mean she had to stay a fool. "I saw enough to know that the two of you set me up," Jill advised Remy and her aunt Hildy coolly. "Or at least you thought you did!"

"Now wait a minute, Jill—" Remy began.

"No, you wait a minute," Jill said furiously, as she poked a finger at Remy's chest. How could he even for one second expect her not to feel betrayed? And yet from the stunned, furious look on his face that was exactly what he expected.

Tears filled her eyes and spilled down her cheeks. "I trusted you! I trusted you both!" She spun away from Remy and glared at her aunt Hildy. "And look where it's gotten me."

"Jill, honey, you don't understand," Hildy began hurriedly as she backed herself into a chair and sat down gingerly on the edge.

"What's not to understand?" Jill shot back sarcastically as she struggled to hold back the tears of hurt and betrayal. Remy had wounded her, but he wasn't going to see her crumple and fall apart.

Jill pointed an accusing finger at her aunt. "You've wanted me to marry again for a long time."

"Well, that's true—" Hildy admitted.

"You also love Remy like a son," Jill continued hotly.

"Also true," Hildy admitted with a perplexed sigh.

Jill scowled at Remy before turning back to her aunt. "Getting Remy and I together, however, was a problem for you, wasn't it? After all, I lived in New York, and he lived here in Louisiana. So the two of you put your heads together and came up with a plan. Aunt Hildy would fake a fall. Remy would rush in to save the day. I'd be called home from New York, for an indefinite period of time during which Remy would be constantly underfoot, both at the house and here at the hospital. You even enlisted Kizzie! Getting me to drink that stupid love potion, making me believe—" Overcome by her feelings of embarrassment and betrayal, Jill whirled and started for the door.

Remy moved to cut her off. Arms folded in front of him, he stood in front of the door handle. "You've got it all wrong, Jill," he warned heavily.

"Oh, have I?" she said sarcastically. "Then why, pray tell, am I the only person here surprised to see my aunt up and walking around today? Are you telling me that you didn't know my aunt's ankle was just fine?" Remy didn't answer Jill, but it wasn't necessary. Jill shook her head in silent bemusement and censure. "That's why you told me not to worry this morning, wasn't it? You knew all along that Aunt Hildy's ankle was just fine!"

Angry tears filling her eyes, Jill whirled on her aunt, then back to Remy. Unable to recall when she had felt so betrayed, she continued softly, putting it all together. "And yesterday, when I came to the hospital and found you two together, Aunt Hildy was up and walking around then, too, wasn't she, Remy?" Jill demanded.

"Yes," Remy admitted reluctantly. His jaw was rigid with displeasure.

"He didn't want to keep it from you, Jill," Hildy interjected.

Jill swung around to face her aunt. "I thought you were different from my father," Jill whispered. "But obviously conning people runs in the family!" She turned back to Remy. "No wonder you get along so well with my aunt! You! My father! My aunt! You're all alike!"

Jill pushed past Remy and reached blindly for the door.

"Jill—" In an effort to stop her, he reached out to touch her arm.

"Back off, Remy," Jill ordered as she shrugged free of his grasp. "I don't want to see or talk to you," she said, feeling as if her heart were breaking. The tears she'd been withholding fell heedlessly down her cheeks. "Not ever again!"

A HUSH FELL IN THE ROOM after Jill departed. Hildy looked at Remy, her own regrets apparent. "Aren't you going to go after her?" she asked, aghast.

Remy shrugged. "You saw her. She's not in the mood to listen to anything either of us say at the moment, and who can blame her?" He scowled out the window, watching for any sign of Jill in the parking lot below. His eyes still trained on her car, Remy sighed. "I should have told her what I'd discovered yesterday, the moment she walked in on us."

"And I should have let her know when my ankle really did stop hurting," Hildy said. Getting back on her feet, she moved to stand beside Remy at the window. "Even so, I can't believe she really thinks so little of us...."

That was the problem; Remy didn't, either.

"She doesn't really believe we conned her," Remy said tiredly. Bitter personal experience had taught him to recognize a woman with one foot out the door when he saw one. "Jill is just looking for excuses to end her relationship with me. She can't say she doesn't love me, so she'll have to find fault with me, somehow make me into this untrustworthy, unlovable person, so, with a clear conscience, she can walk away from what we've found together the past few days."

"You really think that's all this is?" Hildy asked.

"I know it is," Remy said grimly.

Damn it all to hell, he couldn't believe he was in this situation again. Couldn't believe he was involved with a woman who didn't have the courage to be honest with herself, to admit that she was afraid of, or perhaps just unwilling to commit herself to a lifelong relationship. He'd thought this morning, by the way she looked at him, the tender passionate way Jill had made love with him again and again and again, that she was as deeply in love with him as he was with her.

Wishful thinking, Remy thought bitterly as he watched Jill march out of the hospital entrance, across the lot to her car. Nothing was going to matter to Jill except her career. She slammed into her car and took off with a lurch and a squeal. When it came to the long haul, everything else—her aunt, him—would come a very distant second to her career.

"You have to go after her," Hildy said urgently, as Jill's car disappeared from sight. "You have to set her straight."

Remy's lips tightened. "Oh, I intend to have my say, all right," he replied matter-of-factly. Jill needed to know she had no right to be angry with her aunt or with him. As for what happened after . . . that he was less sure about. The Cajun way would be to let the chips fall where they might and accept it as inevitable . . . whereas the fiercely possessive lover in Remy wanted to leave absolutely nothing to chance.

"Well?" Hildy demanded impatiently. "Now what do we do, Remy?"

"*We* will do nothing," Remy corrected. It was past time Hildy removed herself from his and Jill's love life. "I'll give her thirty minutes to calm down, tops, and then she's going to listen to every word I have to say."

"You have to do better than that, Remy. You have to make her believe you," Hildy insisted. "You have to let her know you care, that you would never do anything to hurt her."

Remy looked at Hildy. Hildy was right. He'd come too damn far with Jill to give up now. Their relationship was the best thing that had ever happened to either of them.

It was time to put his Cajun ways aside, and go after what he wanted with everything he had, and what he wanted was Jill. But these were plans he was not going to share with Hildy. This time, Jill was not going to be given the luxury of being tipped off about his intentions.

Remy turned to the beloved neighbor whose caginess had started this all. "I'll handle the anger Jill has directed at me, Hildy. What about you?" Remy asked. "Aren't you worried Jill might not forgive you, either?"

"Oh, pshaw. We'll worry about that later." Her steps slow and measured, Hildy started for the bedside table that housed her personal belongings. "The important thing, Remy, is the two of you." She plucked her handbag out of a drawer, looped it over her arm, and still clad in her robe, flannel pajamas and slippers, sat on the bed to wait. "Now call Dr. Destrehan and get me signed out of here, immediately!"

JILL WAS DRAGGING her suitcases down the stairs when
Remy and Hildy walked in the front door to Magnolia Place. Kizzie walked out to greet them, her black
combat boots ringing on the parquet floor. Kizzie
pointed to Jill. "She's been like that for near on half
an hour!"

"I know," Remy said quietly, looking at Jill. Hand
beneath Hildy's elbow, he escorted Hildy to a chair
and saw her comfortably settled. "You going to be all
right?" he asked gently.

"Kizzie will see I have everything I need," Hildy
said, patting Remy's brawny forearm. "You go on and
take care of things."

Her temper sizzling, Jill arched a brow. Sadly, it
looked like the two of them were still in cahoots.
"Another plan to subdue me?" she asked sweetly.

"No, but looks like we'll need one," Remy muttered.

"Don't flatter yourself!" Jill shot right back.

Kizzie folded her arms in front of her and started to
laugh. "I think I'll take a ringside seat to this one!"

"No need, Kizzie," Remy said. "The show's over.
This one is between Jill and me and no one else!" He
strode over to Jill and stood glowering down at her.
"We need to talk."

Hand to his chest, Jill shoved him aside. "Talk to
yourself," she advised with a haughty toss of her head.

"Ladies, you'll excuse us." Remy slid a hand beneath Jill's knees and swung her up into his arms.

Jill gasped as he stalked out the front door. She had
never seen him in more sober control of himself or his

emotions. "What in blue blazes do you think you are doing?" she demanded condescendingly.

"What I should have done at the hospital."

"Carry me off, caveman-style?"

Remy strode across the grounds of Magnolia Place to his small house next door. "What a novel idea, sugar," he drawled.

Jill's pulse picked up another notch. She didn't know exactly what he had in mind, but she had a feeling getting on her good side and making love to her again very definitely figured into his plans. And she couldn't have that. She had allowed herself to be vulnerable to him once. Never again. "Remy, put me down!"

"Not until you've heard me out," Remy replied flatly.

Jill caught her breath and clung to his neck. She had never seen him like this, so hell-bent on taking charge of the situation—and her. Part of her, the curious part, wanted to give in, to see where this macho behavior of his would lead. The part that had been hurt by the way he and her aunt had conned her into getting involved with him still wanted never to see or speak to him again. "I am listening right now. You do not have to carry me off to Timbuktu, just so we can have a conversation!"

Remy ignored her and kept walking.

She turned her head away from him, taking a strangled breath as she stared out at the meadow of vibrant green that separated their two places. "Remy, I mean it," she warned, every inch of her trembling with a mix of anticipation and anxiety. "Put me down this instant!"

Remy kept going, his strides long, lazy and determined. Jill glared at him, clamped her jaw shut, and fell silent. When they reached his front porch, he did put her down in front of him, but only so he could manage the lock.

"Let go of my waist," Jill said.

Remy smiled at her tightly and continued to hold her close. "I don't think so, sugar."

"Why the hell not?" Jill demanded as he managed the lock with a single twist of the key.

"You know why not," Remy said gruffly, then looked at her as if he'd never met a more impossible, more desirable, more infuriatingly stubborn woman in his life. He opened the door, dropped the hand he'd had on her waist and looked over at her. "Let's try and do this graciously, shall we?"

Jill bit her lip. She didn't want a tussle, either. "If I hear you out, will you leave me alone?"

"I expect you to listen to me. Beyond that, whatever happens between us will be up to you, sugar," he said in a steady, unperturbed voice. His eyes burned into hers. "I'm not in the business of forcing my company on anyone. You have my word on that. Now can we go inside?"

Figuring it would take less time to hear what he had to say than to argue with him, Jill nodded her assent. He walked to the refrigerator, got out the pitcher and two glasses and poured them both a glass of lemonade.

Stalking back, he handed her a glass, then lifted his own to his lips. "I discovered your aunt was able to walk yesterday. Before that, I didn't know."

Jill regarded him silently. Her pulse was tripping along too fast and she wanted so much to believe him. But bitter experience made her wary of any more smoothly uttered lies. She didn't want to be conned by a man. "Then why didn't you tell me that yesterday?" Jill asked.

Remy frowned. "Because she coaxed me not to, and you walked in before I could convince Hildy to come clean with you and Dr. Destrehan. If it makes you feel any better, she said she did it because she wanted to give us time to fall in love. She saw the sparks between us from the very first, and knew, maybe even before we did, that we were meant to be together."

His words made sense. Maybe too much sense. Jill didn't want to think she had fallen victim to her aunt's and Kizzie's matchmaking, but she knew she had. She did love Remy. She just wasn't sure she should. Their involvement had happened so fast. And now given the mixed-up nature of her feelings, she had to wonder whether their passion would last? Did she really want to rearrange her whole life for what could turn out to be no more than a passionate fling?

Still struggling to make sense of all that had happened, Jill said slowly, "What about Kizzie? Where does she fit in to all this?"

Remy drained his glass and set it down on the counter with a thud. "Kizzie did what she did at Hildy's prompting. There was no conspiracy between Kizzie and your aunt and me," he said flatly.

Jill recalled the guilty look on Remy's face when she had walked into the hospital room that morning, the way he had jumped and shoved something into his pocket. More was going on here than he had acknowledged so far. He had been hiding something from her then. She knew it!

"Then why did you look so guilty when I walked in this morning?" Jill asked quietly as she set her glass aside. "Why did you tell my aunt that I wasn't hard to handle at all, and that you had me eating out of your hand? If you two weren't involved in some kind of matchmaking conspiracy, how do you explain any of that?" Jill demanded emotionally.

Remy sighed. "She was teasing me, Jill."

"About the way you had hoodwinked me."

Remy shook his head and shoved a hand through his sandy hair. "About what I was planning," he corrected.

Again, his words had the ring of truth.

Jill's heart thudded all the harder. "And what was that?" she asked as she continued to regard Remy skeptically.

"I was going to ask you to marry me." Remy reached into his jeans pocket and produced a small velvet jeweler's box. "I went to the hospital to show Hildy the ring I bought for you. I wanted her opinion because she's a woman, and I wanted you to like the ring. She started teasing me about my feelings for you, and demanded to know how, when and where I was going to ask you to marry me." He searched her eyes. "You didn't overhear any of that?"

Jill shook her head slowly, her feelings in a jumble as Remy handed her the box. She was happy Remy was so serious, and frightened, too, because if they did decide to get married, she would have to change so much about her life and she wasn't certain she was ready to do that.

With a look at him, she opened the lid, and saw a beautiful solitaire ring nestled in the dark blue velvet. Was it possible she had misjudged them both and made a mountain out of a molehill?

Or was she doing the opposite—overlooking a serious flaw in Remy's character, just because she loved him. She didn't want to be hurt again. She felt she'd already suffered a lifetime of hurt and disillusionment at the hands of her father and her ex-husband.

Her feelings more conflicted than ever, Jill turned away from Remy. Did she really want to give Remy her heart and soul? Was she ready for this?

He followed her to the kitchen window. Though she was still full of doubts, he seemed to have none. While she gripped the sink until her knuckles turned white, Remy said softly, "What you saw this morning, Jill, was merely me showing Hildy the engagement ring I'd bought for you. Hildy was delighted I was so serious about you. And as usual, we started kidding around. She teased me. I teased her back. And that's when you walked in, Jill." Hand on her shoulder, he turned her to face him. "I still had the ring in my hand, so I shoved the box in my pocket and hoped the surprise hadn't been ruined. I just didn't want you to find out my intentions in such an unromantic way. And that's all there was to it. Period."

He snapped the lid on the box shut and put it aside. She had to look away from him or cry.

He caught her hands by the wrists. His voice was low and emotional as he looked into her eyes. "I'm not your father, Jill. I won't make promises I have no intention of keeping and I won't walk out on you. But in return for all that," he said thickly, his beautiful mouth tightening, "I want something, too."

Here it was, Jill thought nervously, the beginning of the demands. Would Remy's be as impossible to meet as her ex-husband's had been? "What?" Jill asked as the pent-up tears spilled down her cheeks.

"I want to know you love me," Remy said hoarsely, tilting her face up to his, and tangling his hands in her hair. "I want to hear you say it. I want to see it in your eyes and feel it in your voice, and the way you kiss...."

"And that's it?" Jill asked thickly.

"That's it," Remy affirmed. "That's all I need from you, Jill—your love."

Jill looked into his eyes and knew it was true. Remy's love for her was unconditional.

Relief flowed through her. She had been right to trust in him and their feelings for each other. She had been right to see past the Cajun charm and to the sweet and tender man inside. "Then how's this for a demonstration of that love?" she asked as she laced her arms about his neck. She kissed him until they were both breathless and yearning, putting all her feelings into the long, passionate embrace.

The next thing she knew they were in his bed. He was kissing her back, pleasing as she pleased. Taking it one day, one moment at a time. They were living life Remy's way, the Cajun way, and there were no more doubts, only sweet fulfillment.

"So...are you still going to ask me to marry you?" Jill asked contentedly a long time later. She wondered how the proposal would have happened, if she hadn't interrupted Remy and her aunt Hildy.

Remy turned, so he was lying on his side, facing her, and gathered her close. He had never looked happier. "That all depends," he murmured lazily as he stroked the profile of her face and looked deep into her eyes. "Do you want to get married? Or would you just be doing it to please me?"

"Does this mean you'd agree to wait if I needed to wait?" Jill said.

"Yep. As long as it takes. Years." He grinned. "Even decades. I'll be here."

She wasn't the only one who had come a long way, Jill thought. Remy had grown a lot, too, in the short time they'd been together. And that, in turn, made her wonder how much they'd progress in the days ahead if they did marry. They certainly brought out the best in each other.

"Well, I appreciate the latitude, Remy," Jill drawled.

"Good."

"But I don't think it'll be necessary for you to wait decades."

His eyes shone with a lazy hope that was also, Jill thought, unbearably sexy. "You don't?" he quipped.

"Nope. Why put off till tomorrow what you can enjoy today?" she teased. As she watched him grin back at her, she went all warm and soft inside. Finally secure in his love, she admitted in all seriousness, "I do want to marry you, Remy. And I want to do it right away. I'm just not sure how it would work," she said slowly, linking hands with him.

"Well, the details are up for grabs," Remy said thoughtfully, stroking her arm from wrist to elbow. "I told Hildy this morning I was willing to relocate my business to New York, and I meant that."

For a moment, Jill was too overwhelmed with emotion to speak. She knew how much Remy loved living in Louisiana, that he had missed the South desperately when he'd been away from it. This was a huge sacrifice on his part. Huge. "You'd do that for me?" she asked in a trembling voice.

Remy nodded, his dark brown eyes serious as he regarded her tenderly. "I'd do anything to make you happy," he said softly.

And suddenly Jill knew everything was going to be all right. Better than all right. "Well, as it happens, I've been doing some thinking and rearranging, too," Jill confessed as she held his hand even tighter. "I called my boss at the network this morning and talked about the possibility of my commuting to New York three to four days a week, and being in Louisiana the rest of the time." Jill took a deep breath. "He said okay."

"You'd keep your job?"

Jill nodded. "And work via fax and phone and perhaps even teleconference on the days when I was here in Louisiana. Which would mean, Remy, that you would not have to relocate to New York permanently. You could stay here. We'd be close to Aunt Hildy and I'd be able to see her a lot more often, too. We could even start a family, if you want."

"Oh, I want, all right," Remy said softly, and as he looked into her eyes Jill thought she knew what utter bliss was like. "Are you sure you won't mind living half your life in one state, and half your life in another?"

Jill rolled so she was on top of him, trapping him beneath her weight. Now that she knew Remy loved her unconditionally, she hadn't a doubt in the world, and it was time Remy knew that, too. "You know what they say about the Cajun way of life," she teased as their bodies molded together and began to heat. "Once it gets in your blood you can't get it out. Well, it's the same for a Cajun man. You're in my blood, Remy, in my heart and in my soul...and I'm never going to get you out. And you know what?" she whispered, pausing to kiss him. "I've stopped wanting to."

They kissed again languidly, then drew apart to catch their breath.

Remy looked at Jill as if all his dreams had just come true. She knew how he felt; she felt the same way. Her world was finally, inevitably right. "Are you absolutely sure you won't mind the travel?" he said as he tangled his hands in her hair.

His concern for her comfort made her smile. "It's a direct flight to New York out of New Orleans," Jill replied. She studied him carefully. "Are you sure you wouldn't mind my being gone a couple days a week?"

"Haven't you heard, sugar? Absence makes the heart grow fonder. Trust me." Remy guided her mouth to his and kissed her once again. "We're going to have some great reunions," he murmured as he paused to trail a line of hot, sexy kisses down her throat.

Jill ran her hands across his shoulders, loving the smooth warm feel of his skin, and the taut muscle beneath. "And if it gets to be too much, being apart even that many days a week?" she asked softly.

"Then I'll hire on as an electrician in New York, part-time, on the days you have to be there," Remy said. "Or maybe even start my own company there, and have two businesses, one in each state. The options are endless, Jill." He rolled so she was beneath him and kissed the curve of her bare shoulder. "We'll work it out, but whatever happens, I won't ask you to give up or cut back on your career. I know how much you love writing for the soaps. I won't ever do anything that would interfere with that."

He really was different from Jake, Jill thought with a sigh of almost overwhelming relief. She'd been right to trust him. Right to love him. Right to care so much about him from the start, even if he did drive her crazy sometimes.

Remy got up, went to the kitchen and returned with the velvet jeweler's box. He snapped open the lid, withdrew the ring and said, "Marry me, Jill."

This once, she didn't even have to think. "Yes."

He fit the ring on her finger, then glanced at her face. "You look happy."

"I am," Jill said.

He kissed her again, languorously, emotionally. "I love you, Jill. I love you with all my heart and soul," he whispered.

And looking into his eyes, Jill knew it was true. She didn't ever have to worry about being abandoned or loved conditionally again. Love Potion #5 or no Love Potion #5, she and Remy had each found their match in one another. And it was a match that would last a lifetime. "I love you, too, Remy Beauregard," she said softly, "with all my heart."

Epilogue

Remy paused in the doorway to Jill's hospital room, drinking in the sight of his wife fussing over their newborn baby girl. Childbirth was supposed to be hard on a woman, yet Jill seemed not only to excel at it, but revel in the entire process.

Her dark hair fluffed out softly around her face and her cheeks were pink with excitement. Her eyes shining with happiness, Jill had never looked more radiant or beautiful than she did at that moment, Remy thought. And as he watched her talking softly to their baby as she changed Lauren's diaper, Remy felt a contentment unlike anything he had ever imagined. This might be domesticity, but it was also magic. Sheer magic . . .

"Where is that silly daddy?" Jill cooed.

"Right here, sugar."

Jill looked up. Her blue eyes sparkled as they met his. "Get everything taken care of in the business office?" she asked.

Remy nodded. "We're all set. We can go home now as soon as you and Lauren are ready."

"We're working on it," Jill promised with a soft laugh as she helped Lauren into a fresh baby-size T-shirt.

Remy walked over to Jill's hospital bed and gazed down at their newborn child. Lauren Beauregard gazed back at both her parents in wide-eyed delight. She might only be three days old, Remy thought, but like her mama, Lauren didn't miss a trick.

"Is it my imagination or does Lauren get prettier with every day that passes?" he said, as he touched Jill's cheek with the back of his hand.

Jill paused to press a light kiss into his palm and look up at Remy affectionately. "I think it's your imagination," she answered dryly, "but for the record, I feel the same way. Lauren is adorable."

"That's because she has her mommy's big blue eyes."

"Her daddy's sandy hair."

"Her mother's cute chin."

"And her father's dazzling grin." Jill finished dressing Lauren then stared at the lone snap she had left. "Whoops! I think I missed a snap somewhere," she murmured, perplexed.

"Here, let me help," Remy said.

Jill sat back on the bed to watch Remy take over the important task of getting Lauren dressed for her very first outing. He handled the snaps on the sleeper like an old pro. She knew he was going to be as wonderful a father to Lauren as he was a husband to her, and her heart swelled with joy.

"So you think Lauren will like riding in the car?" Jill asked. If not, it was going to be a long thirty-minute drive home from the hospital in Baton Rouge.

Remy frowned as he wrapped Lauren in the receiving blanket with Jill's help. "Babies are supposed to really like motion. But just to be on the safe side, I brought the car, rather than the pickup truck. It has a smoother ride."

"Think of everything, don't you?" Jill teased as the nurse brought in the wheelchair.

Remy waggled his eyebrows at Jill as she sat down. He waited until she was settled comfortably, then handed Lauren to her. "I try."

To Jill and Remy's mutual delight, Lauren loved the car. No sooner was she strapped safely into her infant seat, than she was fast asleep.

The peace and quiet jogged Remy's memory. "Oh, before I forget, Patty called this morning. She said not to worry about a thing. She and the producers will handle everything on the set of 'The Brave and the Beautiful' until you get back."

Jill nodded. "Thanks to all the work we did ahead of time on the story lines for next year, everything should go smoothly until my maternity leave is over."

Jill turned to Remy. "When do you have to go back to work?" She had three months off.

"Not until next week. I've got everyone covering for me, in the meantime." He turned the car into the drive. As they approached the house, Jill could see a banner strung across the front porch. It was decorated with pink flowers and lots of greenery and said Welcome Home, Jill and Lauren.

Hildy and Kizzie rushed out to greet them, with Maizie, Frieda and Elanore following swiftly on their heels.

"Welcome home!" they all cried in unison.

Jill got out of the car as Remy lifted Lauren out of her infant seat. The next few moments were consumed by group admiration of their little darling.

"She absolutely is the most beautiful baby ever!" Hildy exclaimed.

Everyone agreed. They continued inside. "I cooked enough meals to last you for a month," Kizzie said shyly. "And I can come over and help you out anytime."

"Thank you, Kizzie," Jill said softly. As she had gotten to know Kizzie better, she had come to like and trust her as much as her aunt did. "I'm sure I'll take you up on that offer."

"Kizzie isn't the only one who gets to baby-sit!" Frieda said. "Maizie, Elanore, Hildy and I are all available. Call us anytime, Jill."

"That'll be a help when I do have to travel to New York," Jill said. Though in the future she was only going to have to go in twice a month, for short periods of time. The rest, they had discovered, could easily be handled by phone, fax and teleconference. In fact, Jill found she was getting more done now that she worked at home most of the time. The network was very pleased.

"And we have another surprise for you," Hildy said. "Remy, since you did most of the work, you get to lead the way."

Remy took Jill's hand, and led her toward the rear of the house where they had been building a studio for Jill and a nursery for Lauren, side by side. "You finished it!" Jill said as she gazed around the sunny, spacious room.

It had only been three-quarters of the way done when she had left for the hospital. Now it was completely outfitted. All the bookshelves were filled. Her office equipment had been installed, her files moved.

"I called in a few markers," Remy explained.

"Thank you," Jill said. She had been dreading putting her studio together, more than he knew.

"And now the nursery..." Hildy said.

Jill walked in and was similarly amazed. When she had left for the hospital, the room had not even been painted. Now the walls were a pale pink. A colorful nursery border had been added, curtains made and hung and the crib and changing table assembled. A comfortable, cushioned rocking chair sat in a corner. There was even a colorful Disney mobile at one end of the crib.

"I don't know what to say," Jill said. "This is all so amazing!"

"We wanted everything to be perfect for you," Maizie said.

"After all," Elanore added, "you are the reason the four of us are so happy now."

"I haven't had so much fun since I lived in a sorority house during college," Frieda said.

Jill knew it had worked out well. Her aunt was happy. So were her friends. Jill saw them all often and knew she could count on any one of them, and vice versa, in a pinch.

In Jill's arms, a sleepy Lauren yawned.

"Ladies, I think that is our signal to vamoose," Hildy said softly.

"You don't have to go," Jill protested.

"You need your rest," Hildy decreed. "And so does Lauren. Not to worry, though. We'll come back to visit tomorrow. Call us, meantime, if you have any problems."

"I will," Jill promised.

She and Remy walked their guests to the door, then returned to the nursery to settle Lauren in her crib. She cuddled up immediately and went right back to sleep. Reluctant to go just yet, Jill and Remy leaned over the crib and watched her. After a few moments, they drifted over to the rocking chair. Remy sat down and pulled Jill onto his lap. She cuddled against him, loving the scent of his cologne and the rugged warmth of his body.

For several moments they rocked together contentedly. Jill marveled at the changes in the past year and cuddled even closer. "Ever wonder what would have happened had we not gotten together?" she asked her husband softly.

"With the powerful Cajun matchmaking forces working to join us in love?" Remy joked. "Impossible."

"I guess you're right," Jill teased back. "Kizzie and my aunt Hildy did do a lot to bring us together."

"Not to mention Gator."

The memory of their trek into the Atchafalaya Swamp brought a smile to Jill's face. "I guess it was one crazy week or two," she said.

"And then some," Remy agreed. He shook his head in silent bemusement as he recalled it. His arm tightened around her, and he dipped his head to nuzzle her neck. "But, just for the record, I never needed anything to heighten my feelings for you. They were there from the very first. As soon as I saw you, I knew you were the woman for me."

"Well, you've got me," Jill said thickly. *For the rest of my life.*

"And you've got me," Remy said as he held her close.

"And we've both got our baby," Jill said. Their arms wrapped around each other, they looked over at Lauren, sleeping peacefully in her crib. "Life couldn't be more perfect," Jill whispered.

Remy hugged her back. "Sugar, I couldn't agree more."

A NEW STAR COMES OUT TO SHINE....

American Romance continues to search
the heavens for the best new talent...
the best new stories.

Join us next month when a new star
appears in the American Romance
constellation:

Mollie Molay
#560 FROM DRIFTER TO DADDY
November 1994

*For sexy bad-boy Quinn Tucker, getting in
trouble with the law wasn't unusual. But
getting "bought" by a gorgeous woman
rancher for a thirty-day parole certainly
was! Could Sara and her twins charm this
drifter into a daddy?*

Be sure to Catch a "Rising Star"!

RISING
STAR

MILLION DOLLAR SWEEPSTAKES (III)

This holiday, join four hunky heroes under
the mistletoe for

Christmas
Kisses

Cuddle under a fluffy quilt, with a cup of hot chocolate and these
romances sure to warm you up:

#561 HE'S A REBEL (also a Studs title)
Linda Randall Wisdom

#562 THE BABY AND THE BODYGUARD
Jule McBride

#563 THE GIFT-WRAPPED GROOM
M.J. Rodgers

#564 A TIMELESS CHRISTMAS
Pat Chandler

Celebrate the season with all four holiday books sealed with a
Christmas kiss—coming to you in December, only from
Harlequin American Romance!

COMING NEXT MONTH

#557 ONCE UPON A HONEYMOON by Julie Kistler

Self-proclaimed bachelor Tripp Ashby was in a no-win situation...and only Bridget Emerick could help him. His old pal had bailed him out since college—but this time, the sexy bachelor needed the unthinkable...a wife! *Don't miss the second book in the STUDS miniseries!*

#558 QUINN'S WAY by Rebecca Flanders

Heartbeat

When David Quinn appeared out of nowhere and entered Houston Malloy's ordered life—mouthwatering smile, bedroom eyes and all—she thought the man was out of this world. Little did she know how right she was!

#559 SECRET AGENT DAD by Leandra Logan

As a secret agent, Michael Hawkes had stared down danger with nerves of steel. But then he found himself protecting his old flame Valerie Warner—and her twins—in the jungles of suburbia. Twins who looked an awful lot like him.... Michael never saw danger like he did now!

#560 FROM DRIFTER TO DADDY by Mollie Molay

Rising Star

For a couple of hundred bucks Sara Martin bought the wrongfully imprisoned drifter Quinn Tucker for thirty days. But it didn't take long for Quinn to know he was safer in jail, doing his time, than he was out on a ranch with a gorgeous woman and her ready-made family....

AVAILABLE THIS MONTH:

#553 THE MARRYING TYPE
Judith Arnold

#554 THE INVISIBLE GROOM
Barbara Bretton

#555 FINDING DADDY
Judy Christenberry

#556 LOVE POTION #5
Cathy Gillen Thacker

 HARLEQUIN ®  Silhouette®

The movie event of the season can be the reading event of the year!

Lights... The lights go on in October when CBS presents Harlequin/Silhouette Sunday Matinee Movies. These four movies are based on bestselling Harlequin and Silhouette novels.

Camera... As the cameras roll, be the first to read the original novels the movies are based on!

Action... Through this offer, you can have these books sent directly to you! Just fill in the order form below and you could be reading the books...before the movie!

48288-4	Treacherous Beauties by Cheryl Emerson		
	$3.99 U.S./$4.50 CAN.	☐
83305-9	Fantasy Man by Sharon Green		
	$3.99 U.S./$4.50 CAN.	☐
48289-2	A Change of Place by Tracy Sinclair		
	$3.99 U.S./$4.50CAN.	☐
83306-7	Another Woman by Margot Dalton		
	$3.99 U.S./$4.50 CAN.	☐

TOTAL AMOUNT	$	
POSTAGE & HANDLING	$	
($1.00 for one book, 50¢ for each additional)		
APPLICABLE TAXES*	$_____	
TOTAL PAYABLE	$_____	
(check or money order—please do not send cash)		

To order, complete this form and send it, along with a check or money order for the total above, payable to Harlequin Books, to: **In the U.S.:** 3010 Walden Avenue, P.O. Box 9047, Buffalo, NY 14269-9047; **In Canada:** P.O. Box 613, Fort Erie, Ontario, L2A 5X3.

Name: _____

Address: _____ City: _____

State/Prov.: _____ Zip/Postal Code: _____

*New York residents remit applicable sales taxes.
Canadian residents remit applicable GST and provincial taxes.

CBSPR

"HOORAY FOR HOLLYWOOD" SWEEPSTAKES

HERE'S HOW THE SWEEPSTAKES WORKS

OFFICIAL RULES — NO PURCHASE NECESSARY

To enter, complete an Official Entry Form or hand print on a 3" x 5" card the words "HOORAY FOR HOLLYWOOD", your name and address and mail your entry in the pre-addressed envelope (if provided) or to: "Hooray for Hollywood" Sweepstakes, P.O. Box 9076, Buffalo, NY 14269-9076 or "Hooray for Hollywood" Sweepstakes, P.O. Box 637, Fort Erie, Ontario L2A 5X3. Entries must be sent via First Class Mail and be received no later than 12/31/94. No liability is assumed for lost, late or misdirected mail.

Winners will be selected in random drawings to be conducted no later than January 31, 1995 from all eligible entries received.

Grand Prize: A 7-day/6-night trip for 2 to Los Angeles, CA including round trip air transportation from commercial airport nearest winner's residence, accommodations at the Regent Beverly Wilshire Hotel, free rental car, and $1,000 spending money. (Approximate prize value which will vary dependent upon winner's residence: $5,400.00 U.S.); 500 Second Prizes: A pair of "Hollywood Star" sunglasses (prize value: $9.95 U.S. each). Winner selection is under the supervision of D.L. Blair, Inc., an independent judging organization, whose decisions are final. Grand Prize travelers must sign and return a release of liability prior to traveling. Trip must be taken by 2/1/96 and is subject to airline schedules and accommodations availability.

Sweepstakes offer is open to residents of the U.S. (except Puerto Rico) and Canada who are 18 years of age or older, except employees and immediate family members of Harlequin Enterprises, Ltd., its affiliates, subsidiaries, and all agencies, entities or persons connected with the use, marketing or conduct of this sweepstakes. All federal, state, provincial, municipal and local laws apply. Offer void wherever prohibited by law. Taxes and/or duties are the sole responsibility of the winners. Any litigation within the province of Quebec respecting the conduct and awarding of prizes may be submitted to the Regie des loteries et courses du Quebec. All prizes will be awarded; winners will be notified by mail. No substitution of prizes are permitted. Odds of winning are dependent upon the number of eligible entries received.

Potential grand prize winner must sign and return an Affidavit of Eligibility within 30 days of notification. In the event of non-compliance within this time period, prize may be awarded to an alternate winner. Prize notification returned as undeliverable may result in the awarding of prize to an alternate winner. By acceptance of their prize, winners consent to use of their names, photographs, or likenesses for purpose of advertising, trade and promotion on behalf of Harlequin Enterprises, Ltd., without further compensation unless prohibited by law. A Canadian winner must correctly answer an arithmetical skill-testing question in order to be awarded the prize.

For a list of winners (available after 2/28/95), send a separate stamped, self-addressed envelope to: Hooray for Hollywood Sweepstakes 3252 Winners, P.O. Box 4200, Blair, NE 68009.

CBSRLS

OFFICIAL ENTRY COUPON

"Hooray for Hollywood"
SWEEPSTAKES!

Yes, I'd love to win the Grand Prize — a vacation in Hollywood — or one of 500 pairs of "sunglasses of the stars"! Please enter me in the sweepstakes!

This entry must be received by December 31, 1994.
Winners will be notified by January 31, 1995.

Name _____

Address _____ Apt. _____

City _____

State/Prov. _____ Zip/Postal Code _____

Daytime phone number _____
                                    (area code)

Mail all entries to: Hooray for Hollywood Sweepstakes, P.O. Box 9076, Buffalo, NY 14269-9076.
In Canada, mail to: Hooray for Hollywood Sweepstakes, P.O. Box 637, Fort Erie, ON L2A 5X3.

KCH

OFFICIAL ENTRY COUPON

"Hooray for Hollywood"
SWEEPSTAKES!

Yes, I'd love to win the Grand Prize — a vacation in Hollywood — or one of 500 pairs of "sunglasses of the stars"! Please enter me in the sweepstakes!

This entry must be received by December 31, 1994.
Winners will be notified by January 31, 1995.

Name _____

Address _____ Apt. _____

City _____

State/Prov. _____ Zip/Postal Code _____

Daytime phone number _____
                                    (area code)

Mail all entries to: Hooray for Hollywood Sweepstakes, P.O. Box 9076, Buffalo, NY 14269-9076.
In Canada, mail to: Hooray for Hollywood Sweepstakes, P.O. Box 637, Fort Erie, ON L2A 5X3.

KCH